RED CARD

STEPHEN D. SMITH with LISE CALDWELL

Standard®
PUBLISHING
Bringing The Word to Life

Cincinnati, Ohio

From Stephen

For Mr. B., my Junior High language arts teacher,
for encouraging me to write when I only
liked to draw.

From Lise

For Jack and Will

ISBN-13: 978-0-7847-1438-6
ISBN-10: 0-7847-1438-X

11 10 09 08 07   9 8 7 6 5 4 3 2

CHAPTER:01

A shrill whistle pierced the early April morning. The dew on the Cedar Brook, Oklahoma, district soccer field had finally evaporated, but a low mist still hugged the tops of the nearby trees. Paul Stewart and the other Cedar Brook Saints crouched, ready to sprint to the opposite goal. The coach blew his whistle again, and Paul, along with his teammates, dashed down field. Paul's brother Andy quickly outpaced everyone.

Andy and Paul were twins, but no one ever believed it. Paul was short and thin, with dark, straight hair and dark olive skin. Andy was several inches taller, with curly red hair, light skin, and freckles. Broad and strong, most people thought Andy was at least two years older than Paul, rather than two minutes. He even had to shave already—not very often, but still. Paul checked the mirror every morning for signs of facial hair, but so far, nothing. The only thing they had in common was the same color eyes: almond brown.

This was the first time in three years the two of them had played soccer together. When Paul was a kid, people always used to ask him what it was like to have a twin.

"I don't know," he'd say. "What's it like not to have one?"

Paul never imagined life without Andy. They'd had a great time together, building forts, playing soccer, shooting hoops. What kid wouldn't want to have a best friend right there all the time? Sure, they'd fought over toys and trading cards, but for the most part, things had been great.

But about three years ago, something changed. Paul was still trying to figure out what. All he knew was that Andy wasn't fun anymore. Everything was a big competition, and Paul was always on the losing side. So Paul told his mom he didn't like soccer and didn't want to play anymore. His dad was mad, but his mom stuck up for him.

"I've just grown out of it," he told his mom, making sure Andy could hear.

But he hadn't. He still loved soccer. He was just tired of being compared to Andy all the time. This year, though, Paul had decided to give it another try. Seventh grade was the last year he could play at this level of park league soccer. After that, tryouts got even tougher. So Paul convinced himself he could do it. After all, soccer wasn't just about physical strength. It was about strategy and skill. Paul studied and practiced on his own, and, without telling Andy, went out for the soccer team. He made it.

And now, here he was on another Saturday morning, watching his taller, red-headed twin brother sprint past him. Coach Benedict was really big on wind sprints. Some days, Paul was really big on yanking the whistle off of Coach Benedict's neck. Instead, he just ran harder.

"Come on Stewart, pick up the pace," the coach yelled.

Paul knew immediately which Stewart the coach meant. Andy, already across the field, looked back at Paul and smirked.

Go ahead and laugh, moron, Paul thought. *You may be able to run, but I can get my offensive line in formation. I can score.* If only Coach would remember that.

A minute later the whistle sounded, and the team sprinted back across the field again. Again Paul pushed himself as Andy ran past him in a blur. Paul's brother had already turned and was heading back before Paul had even reached the other side of the field. Paul hated these kinds of practices. He turned to his friend Mitch Berry, who was about the same size as Paul, panting next to him.

"Do you remember when we used to actually use

a soccer ball at soccer practice?"

"Soccer ball?" Mitch grunted. "What's a soccer ball?"

"Okay, guys," said Coach Benedict. "Good practice. See you next week."

"I'm so thirsty, but I don't think I can move," Mitch said, sitting down on the grass field. Sweat dripped from his short, light-brown hair into eyes the color of greenish-blue seawater. When he smiled, his cheeks dimpled, making it hard for his mother to resist any request.

"Hey, Paul."

"Yeah?"

"Would you go get my water bottle?"

"Uh, no." Paul lay back on the cushion of green grass, too tired to walk to the sidelines for his own water bottle. Mitch was really Paul's only friend on the team. The other guys all wanted to hang out with Andy.

"If we wait here long enough, maybe the sprinklers will come on," Paul added. "Then we can just open our mouths and let the water fall in."

Paul closed his eyes, and he suddenly felt cooler. A cloud must have blocked out the harsh sun, which had beat down today with unusual force for early spring.

"Hey, Sis." That was no cloud. It was Andy. Slowly, Paul opened one eye. "What's the matter?" Andy asked. "All worn out, Paula?"

"Take a hike, Android," Paul said.

"Don't worry. Mommy's on her way with a cold drink of water for her itsy-witsy baby." Andy laughed and walked away, saying, "Hey, Dad. You should have been here today! You won't believe the time I set—"

"Hey, Andy! Who's the shrimp?" Paul knew Jimmy was referring to him. He ignored the remark and considered the source.

Jimmy Hong was Andy's best friend. Some kids called him Crash because of the way he "crashed" smaller guys into soft drink and candy bar vending machines to get free stuff.

"Nobody," Andy said, walking away from his brother.

Paul sat up as his mom approached. Everybody said Paul looked just like her, and Andy looked just like Dad. Not exactly two peas in a pod. Mom handed Paul and Mitch each a bottle of water.

"Thanks, Mrs. Stewart."

"Yeah, thanks Mom," Paul said, chugging down half the bottle.

"It's just too hot out here," she said. "You boys shouldn't be practicing in this heat wave. It's not safe."

"It's okay, Mom," Paul said. "It's only April."

"Still, it's hot," she said. "Paulie, are you up for Taco Casa?"

Mitch smirked, flashing his dimples, and mouthed *Paulie*. Paul punched his buddy on the arm and said, "Sounds great, Mom."

"Would you like to join us, Mitch?" she asked.

"No thanks, Mrs. Stewart. I've got to help my mom set up for my little brother's birthday party," he said. "He wanted a pirate theme, so I have to figure out how to make him an eye patch."

Paul's dad yelled across the field, "Come on, Theresa!"

"In a minute!" she called back. "Paul's resting."

"Tell him to suck it up," Dad yelled. "Andy and I are starving!"

Paul remained quiet on the way to Taco Casa. Andy rattled on to Dad all about practice, and how great everything had been—for Andy. Paul stared out the window. They passed his mom's favorite restaurant, Kountry Kabin Kooking. He had always wondered why businesses felt compelled to intentionally misspell their names.

By the time they got to Taco Casa, Paul was starving. He ordered his usual—trés tacos with extra guacamole. After washing his hands, he slid into the booth next to Andy just in time to see Andy and their dad pouring extra-firey hot sauce all over their food.

"Want some?" Andy asked, looking at Paul knowing very well what Paul's answer would be.

"No thanks," he said. The last time Andy and Dad had talked him into trying hot sauce, his tongue had burned for three days. "I don't know how you to stand that stuff."

"It'll put hair on your chest," his dad said.

"Maybe that's why Andy looks like an orangutan," Paul muttered. Andy punched him in the thigh.

"That's enough, Paul," his dad said.

Paul opened his mouth to respond and then closed it again. It was pointless to argue. His dad always took Andy's side.

Mom arrived, carrying four tall glasses of iced tea, and set them down just like a real waitress.

"So," she said. "How was practice?"

"Great!" said Andy.

"Okay," said Paul.

"What's wrong, Paul?" his mom asked.

"Nothing. It's just that when I signed up to play soccer this year, I was under the impression I might actually get to play soccer instead of run wind sprints up and down the field."

"What's wrong, midget? Practice too hard for you?" Andy sneered. "Coach Benedict is the best coach in the district. A little running now and then won't kill you."

"Now, Andy," Mom said. "Paul isn't in the same shape as you. You need to make allowances."

"Theresa, that's the boy's problem," Dad said. "You've made 'allowances,' for Paul all his life. No wonder he can barely run across a soccer field."

Paul didn't know which he hated more: the way his mom stood up for him or the way his dad insulted him. Either way, they all knew Andy was the athletic one—stronger, braver, and better at almost every sport.

In the noisy Mexican restaurant, their table was silent except for the sound of crunching taco shells. Paul drained his iced tea and got up to refill his glass. When he came back, he took a bite of his third taco.

"Ahhhh!!! Hot sauce!" he gasped. "Water! Water!"

Andy was laughing so hard, his face turned red under his freckles, and he had to hold his stomach.

"You think that's funny?" Paul asked. "You would, you Neanderthal ostrich brain!"

"Paul, we don't insult each other in this family," his father said sternly. "Apologize to your brother."

Paul's mouth was on fire, and now that feeling of heat spread through his body. He was angrier than he'd ever been. Andy always got away with everything. Now, somehow, this was Paul's fault too. He hated that his eyes were watering. It was from the hot sauce, but he knew Andy would think he was crying.

"Apologize," his father repeated.

Paul turned to Andy. "I'm sorry I called you a Neanderthal ostrich brain," he said out loud. Under his breath he added, "It was an insult to ostriches everywhere." Paul could tell Andy heard him, but his parents didn't, and surprisingly, Andy kept his mouth shut.

"And Andy, you apologize for dumping hot sauce on Paul's taco," Mom said sternly.

"Sorry, Paulie," Andy said. "I should have remembered you couldn't take it."

When they got home, Paul hauled up his scuffed, navy-blue backpack on the kitchen table and pulled out his earth science textbook. He had a project due next Friday, and he wanted to get a head start on it.

Paul glanced up and watched Andy plop down in front of the TV in the family room, with the remote in one hand and a sports drink in the other. Their cable package came with about six different sports channels, and Andy and their dad spent most of every weekend surfing from one to another. That is, when they weren't out kicking the ball. Or hiking. Or camping. Andy and their dad were more like friends than father and son.

Paul had always felt closer to his mom. Partly because his dad was gone with work so much, and partly because he liked taking care of her. He loved doing his homework at the kitchen table while she cooked. The smell of peppers, onions, and garlic sau-téed in olive oil filled that room almost every night.

His father's family originated in Scotland, and his dad had spent his childhood in Manchester, England, before moving to the States when he was eight.

His mom, though, was from a large Italian family. Her garden boasted six different kinds of tomatoes and ten different kinds of peppers. She canned her own marinara sauce and all the neighbors begged for it at Christmastime. The kitchen was her world, and Paul wondered if she ever really saw what was happening outside of it—like the way Andy always treated Paul.

"What's on your mind, Paulie?" his mom asked.

"Huh?" he said, startled.

"You've been staring into space for ten minutes," she said.

He wondered if he should even bother to explain. "Do you remember when Andy and I were friends?" he asked.

"What are you talking about, Paul? You and your brother have always been friends."

Which was exactly what Paul thought she would say.

"Come on, Mom," he said. "We used to get along. We even had fun together. Now he'd just as soon punch me out as look at me. He hates me, Mom."

"Oh, honey, that's just not true. You and Andy are twins—"

"Yeah," Paul interrupted. "Or so you keep telling me."

"And that means you share a bond deeper than most people can understand," she finished, ignoring him.

"So does that mean he can make me his punching bag, and I'm supposed to see that as brotherly affection?"

"I think maybe you're a little too hard on Andy," Mom said.

"Me?" Paul asked. He couldn't believe what she'd said. "I'm too hard on *him*?"

"It's okay, Paulie. Don't get so upset."

Paul knew it was pointless to continue the conversation. His mom hated anyone getting upset. She'd rather leave the house than fight with Dad. And Paul could tell, he was upsetting her.

"I'm not upset," he said.

"Good. Can I make you a sandwich?" she asked.

Mom thought the world's problems could be fixed by food.

"No thanks," Paul said. "I'm still full from Taco Casa."

That night, Paul lay awake for awhile, listening to Andy snore in the bed next to his. *What was I thinking, signing up to play soccer this year?*

He remembered the first time he and Andy went to a soccer practice. They were seven, and Andy was terrified. Paul held Andy's hand and stuck with him all through practice. Back then, the two of them were harder to tell apart, and the coach always got them confused. Once, when Andy kicked the ball into the wrong goal, the coach had yelled at him.

"Come on, Andy!" he said, frustrated. "What were you thinking?"

Paul had yelled from across the field. "I'm Andy! That's Paul." Paul didn't want Andy to feel bad. After that the coach always thought Paul was the one who made the bad plays.

Later that season, he remembered hearing the coach tell his dad, "Andy, well, he's got real potential. Paul on the other hand—don't count on any soccer scholarships for him."

At the time, Paul thought it was funny, and he was glad his plan to help Andy had worked so well. Now he wondered if that's when things between them had gone bad.

Before he drifted off to sleep, Paul prayed, "Dear God, please make it right between Andy and me. I don't want to hate my brother, but he's such a jerk. Sorry, God, but you know what I mean. In Jesus' name, Amen."

Sunday mornings at the Stewart house were filled with chaos and shouting. Paul never could figure out how they all managed to get dressed and leave the house Monday through Friday without much problem, but on Sundays they were always ten minutes late getting in the car and yelled at each other all the way to church.

Andy hated church. He said it was boring. When they were kids, Paul and Andy had always attended Sunday school, Vacation Bible School, and church camp together. But about three years ago, Andy started complaining about everything. Gradually, he dropped out of every church activity, except the main service on Sunday morning. And that was only because Mom made him go. Paul thought maybe that was why Andy always treated him worse on Sundays.

Andy shoved Paul out of the way before Paul could slide in behind Dad. Mom and Dad had tuned out the twins, because Dad was doing his usual complaining about being late. So when Andy punched Paul in the arm—hard—after they got in the van, Paul knew better than to say anything.

Although Paul hated the ride to church, he really enjoyed being there afterward because of their youth minister, Will Chandler. Paul thought Will was really cool—not anything like what he expected a minister to be. Will worked out with weights, ran in marathons, and was great at sports. He'd passed up a football scholarship to a big state school to go to Bible college instead.

But what Paul liked best about him was how kind he was. Will was always telling jokes, but he never made fun of anyone. Oh, he might tease you, but not in a hurtful way. He took the kids on lots of missions trips. Paul always felt like a nicer person when he'd spent time around Will.

His mom and dad wanted the boys to go to "big church" now instead of the youth service, so they could be together as a family. He didn't mind too much, but the sermons weren't that interesting. Not that Pastor Jamison was a bad preacher. He just talked about stuff that didn't have much to do with Paul's life—like how to raise your kids and be a good neighbor and stuff.

Paul thought if Andy would come to youth group, too, he might not think church was so boring. But frankly, for Paul one of the best things about church was that Andy wasn't always there. Paul could just be Paul instead of "Andy's twin."

As the Stewart family edged their way through the crowd toward the sanctuary, Paul spotted Rachel Cassidy. Rachel was in seventh grade, too, but she went to a different school. She had long, light-brown hair that fell around her shoulders—straight and shiny. Paul thought she always smelled like vanilla.

"Hey, Paul, you coming to youth group tonight?" Rachel asked.

"Wouldn't miss it!" Paul said.

She turned to Andy. "Hey, Red, what about you?"

"No way!" Andy snorted like it was the lamest suggestion he'd ever heard. Paul was a little ashamed of himself for feeling so relieved that Andy said no.

After the service, Dad and Andy hustled them all to the parking lot because Dad's favorite soccer team, Manchester United, was playing Liverpool and the game was being televised. Usually, they went out to lunch after church, which was really the main reason Andy agreed to attend church at all.

At home, Andy plopped down on the couch as his dad grabbed the remote. Paul stood behind them, trying to decide if he should watch the game or finish his homework. He enjoyed watching soccer, because he always learned some new strategies. But he hated listening to Andy scream at the players and the refs. Dad clicked on the TV. Liverpool was one of Manchester's big rivals, and the fans were already going crazy in the stands.

"Look at those people!" Paul laughed. "In America, soccer is a sport. In England, it's a disease."

"You're the disease," Andy said. "And besides, they don't call it soccer over there. They call it football."

"Thanks for the info, Genius. I know that," Paul said.

Dad had kicked back in the recliner, and Andy was stretched out on the couch, so Paul flopped down in the chair Mom usually sat in.

He couldn't wait to see what Manchester's Kevin Eubank, the team captain, would do today. Paul understood Kevin Eubank. He and Paul were in the game for the same reasons. Strategy. Winning by calculated plays. Andy just liked to see guys get creamed. The rougher the game, the more fun it was for Paul's brother. But that wasn't Paul's style. Or Kevin Eubank's.

Eubank was the master of the foot trap. He could stop a ball with his foot and have control of it within a fraction of a second. Once he possessed the ball and the team went into an attack formation, there was no stopping them.

"Come on, Eubank!" his dad yelled.

"And goal! Whoo-hoo!" Andy jumped up from the sofa, and he and his dad gave each other a high-five. Then he flopped down again.

"Hey, Paulie. Chips!" Andy said, without even looking at his brother.

"Why, certainly," Paul said, sarcastically. "I'd be delighted to pass you the chips. Thank you for asking so politely."

"Whatever," Andy said, grabbing the chip bowl.

When Paul was sure his brother was riveted by the

game, he took out a pad of paper and started taking notes. He wanted to learn all he could from Eubank.

Suddenly, Andy yelled, "Look at DiSanto. He's going after the goalie!"

Paul turned toward the screen and saw that a fight was about to break out on the field. Andy was halfway off the sofa, when he yelled, "Clobber him!"

"Settle down, tiger," Dad said to Andy.

Paul was surprised. Generally, their dad never got on Andy's case about anything. Andy thought the rougher the game, the more exciting it was.

"What?" Andy said absentmindedly and turned back to the TV to find out the fight had been broken up quickly and with only a yellow-card warning. "Bummer."

It turned out to be an exciting match. With only two minutes left in the game, Liverpool had come back from behind and was leading 6 to 5. Manchester managed to gain possession of the ball. A player kicked a center pass from just before the middle sideline and was intercepted by another teammate positioned in the forward third of the field. He in turn made a wing-cross kick to Eubank, who was waiting at the opposite side of the goal from the goalkeeper. He kicked it in. The score was now tied and while the Manchester team was giving it their all, there was little time to score again unless the game ended in a tie.

The ball was in the possession of Liverpool, who held a tight 3-3-4 formation as they moved toward the defending goal. With four players moving toward the goal, unified by the drive to score one more point, Liverpool took control of the game. Three midfielders and three defenders stayed back as the four teammates in forward positions went on the attack. As the ball was kicked toward Manchester's goal, the goalie watched its approach and deflected it with a painful looking scissor kick.

One of the Liverpool forwards lunged into the goal area and took the full force of the goalkeeper's kick to the side of his head. Everyone in the stadium and the Stewart's family room held their collective breath. The ball bounced off the falling player and into the net, making the game a victory for Liverpool.

As the Liverpool forward lay motionless on the ground, Paul and his dad watched to see if he would be okay.

"Way to go, Manchester," said Andy. "That guy deserved to be knocked down."

On the screen, medics ran onto the field as the camera switched to a close-up of the limp player, whose face was covered in blood. As Paul and his dad watched intently, another camera angle showed a growing brawl in the stands, no doubt between rival fans. Players on both teams were concerned. Some stood around the downed player, while others stared up at the growing turmoil in the grandstands.

"I sure hope he's okay," Paul said quietly. He glanced over at his dad, who was looking not at the screen, but at Andy. Dad's face was filled with concern.

Paul walked out of the room, taking the snacks his mom had made for the game back to the kitchen, leaving his brother to enjoy the spectacle of blood.

CHAPTER:02

Paul hated lunchtime. Walking with his tray clenched tightly in his hands, he looked around for a seat in the crowded cafeteria. He knew some kids looked forward to lunch, because it was a break from class. Not Paul. When he was in class, Paul felt confident. He did really well in school, and during class, even the cool kids were nice to him because they wanted his help. The cafeteria was a completely different arena, and he was fresh meat.

Once in Mr. Wallace's social studies class, Paul had learned about the law of the jungle, where the strong survive and the weak are an afternoon snack. That's what Paul felt like in the cafeteria—an afternoon snack for the school's strongest predators…the popular kids. Too many times, Paul had been the victim of "accidental" bumps that landed chicken noodle soup or chocolate pudding all over his shirt. Too many chairs had been pulled out from underneath him. For Paul, lunch was a time to survive, not thrive.

Finally, Paul spotted some of his friends at a table across the cafeteria. They waved. As he passed Andy, ignoring him, Paul saw a foot snaking out from under the table. He carefully maneuvered around it. Even in the jungle, the weak can survive by being smart.

Paul set down his tray on the brown, folding table and slid in next to Gavin Hooper, one of his best friends. Stephen Landau and Topher Goldstein sat across from them. Last year, Paul had been on the academic team with these guys. In fact, they *were* the academic team. But Paul had quit this year so he could play soccer.

"Did any of you see the Manchester/Liverpool game yesterday?" Paul asked as he sat down.

"The whaty-who?" Gavin asked.

"We had a match against Central Middle School yesterday," Stephen reminded him.

"Oh, yeah," Paul said. "How was it?"

"Torture," Topher said. "Gavin covered math and Stephen and I did well with history, but they killed us in social studies. We could have used you there."

Here we go again, thought Paul.

"Tell me, please, why you chose to play soccer this year—" Gavin began.

"For which you get almost no playing time—" Stephen added.

"And during which you have to spend time with

your evil twin brother—" Topher jumped in.

"Instead of staying on the academic team, where you were unstoppable?" Gavin finished.

Paul was beginning to wonder the same thing. They were right. He never got to play. Plus he had to spend more time around Andy, who was always giving him grief, rather than hanging out with his own friends.

But even with these guys, Paul didn't feel like he could always be himself. He got along great with them when they were debating politics or talking about the latest *National Geographic* article. But they all hated sports. Gavin called sports "the last refuge of idiots," and Paul could never get them to see how you could use your intelligence to be a better player.

He didn't feel like talking about Kevin Eubank again, or trying to explain for the thousandth time why soccer was so important to him.

"Let's just eat and get to gym," Paul said.

"Goody," said Gavin sarcastically. He pushed his glasses up on his nose. "My favorite class."

Because of warm spring weather, gym class was now held in the field behind the middle school. A baseball diamond, surrounded by a chain-link fence, anchored the far corner of the field. The rest of the grass was marked off for soccer and field events.

The new mint-colored grass had been cut over the weekend, and fresh marking lines had been painted.

Paul scanned the field, but his attention strayed to the mammoth water tower across the street, which was surrounded by scaffolding. The tank was getting a fresh coat of white paint by city workers to remove the graffiti that had slowly covered its surface during the year. Paul wondered how safe it was to stand up there. The scaffolding looked as flimsy as some of his construction toys he had put together as a kid. Coach Taylor's whistle brought Paul back to reality.

"All right guys, we're going to spend another week on soccer before we move into track. When I call your name alphabetically, I'll split you up into two teams: A and B. Anderson…A, Albright…B, Berkowitz…A, Crosby…B." Although it made some of the guys mad to divide the teams this way, Paul always liked it because it meant he never had to be on Andy's team.

Andy, Jimmy "Crash" Hong, and Tim Howard, who also played on the Saints, huddled up with the other guys picked for the A team. Jimmy and Tim were as big as Andy and looked more like eighth graders. Paul noticed Andy immediately took control of the group and shouted instructions at them.

Go ahead, Paul thought. *This might get interesting.*

Paul and his team, which included Gavin, Topher, and Stephen, huddled with the B team. Paul waited for someone to assume the leadership role, but realized they were all looking to him for guidance.

"What do you want me to do?" he asked.

"Here's your chance, Mr. Soccer," Gavin said. "You're always telling us that soccer is more about brains that brute strength. Show us."

A smile spread across Paul's face. "You got it."

Paul explained some basic formation strategies to outwit the larger players on the other team, knowing perfectly well that Andy would be targeting him personally. Paul kept checking his brother's huddle to see if he could read their body language. The last time he looked over, Andy sneered back at him.

Paul's team won the kickoff and quickly set up the formation Paul had described for them. Paul ran forward to the sideline near the corner. If his teammates could just move the ball, he would be able to score. Out of the corner of his eye, he saw his brother running to block him. Paul's eyes flashed back and forth between blonde Cory Albright, who readied to make a chip pass to him, and his red-headed brother Andy, who's superior weight barreled toward him.

As Paul positioned himself to receive the pass, Topher ran across right behind him and threw the charging Andy off balance. *Good job, Topher! You were listening.* Paul connected with the ball and like Kevin Eubank, made a breakaway attack on the goalie. He kicked the ball directly into the net.

"Score for the B team! Good job, Stewart!" the

coach called out. This time, Paul was glad the "Stewart" was him. If only Coach Benedict were here right now.

The A team possessed the ball now. Andy and his goons charged with it straight down the field. Paul noticed Andy's team was all over the place and that Andy and Crash were exclusively handling the ball.

Evidently, the coach noticed, too. "Stewart, Hong, work with the rest of your team," he called out, prompting Andy to pass the ball to a kid who immediately passed it back.

They made it past midfield and were charging the goal, when Paul signaled Gavin to distract Jimmy "Crash" Hong. Gavin, not exactly sure what to do, ran directly to Hong, throwing his concentration off of the other guards. This allowed Paul to take position as another of his teammates again ran from off-side to kick the ball out of Andy's control, straight to Paul, who was able to kick a long power shot into the net. Jumping up and down, the B team surrounded Paul.

"You're really on to something!" said Gavin. Paul's friend slapped him so hard on the back it almost took his breath away. "Brains are an advantage in this game!"

For the duration of the game, Paul managed to keep his brother off balance and guessing at his moves. But best of all, Paul's team won the match. Andy was not a happy camper, but Paul didn't care. His brother glared at him before stomping toward the locker room.

Coach Taylor pulled Paul aside.

"You're really good out there, Paul," Coach said. "Have you ever thought of going out for park league soccer like your brother?"

"I played for years," he said. "And I'm back at it this season. But thanks."

Paul walked back into the school, knowing that Andy would find a way to get revenge for his victory. Paul would have to watch his back.

As Paul stepped into the locker room and headed for his locker, Andy waited for him. Paul tried to push past, but Andy blocked him with his hand.

"What?" Paul said impatiently.

"How come you're trying to make me look bad on the field?" Andy asked.

"What do you mean? Just because my team won? Not everything is about you, Andy. We were better. We worked together, and we beat you. Maybe you should think about that and use my skills, instead of always trying to make me look bad at soccer practice. We might chalk up a few wins there too."

Paul pushed Andy's arm out of the way and walked through toward his locker.

After Paul changed, he headed to math class, but didn't see his twin brother again until after school. Usually they took the bus home, but both boys had orthodontist appointments that afternoon so Mom planned to pick them up. They ignored each other until she pulled up in her dark green minivan, and then both boys headed for the front passenger seat. Paul reached the handle first, but Andy shoved him out of the way and climbed in next to Mom.

"You two act like a couple of five-year-olds," she said.

Paul slid into the back seat, threw his backpack down next to him, and pulled the large panel door closed. He was steaming. Not just over this, but because he knew Andy wouldn't forget what had happened on the soccer field during gym class. He knew Andy would make him pay.

Paul waited all week for Andy to seek revenge, but nothing happened. Nothing unusual that is. Andy continued to punch or trip him whenever he could.

"Just kidding," Andy would joke, but for Paul the punch line was getting old. He was really tired of having to watch his back, especially since they slept in the same room. At night, Paul always checked his bed for booby-traps and would wait until Andy started snoring before he allowed himself to doze off.

But during the day, Paul was the new hero among the kids who didn't belong to the popular group. Thanks to Gavin, Stephen, and Topher, who treated him with new respect, word of their gym soccer victory had spread throughout the school. And his buddies gave Paul full credit for the win.

"You were right," Gavin told him, cleaning his glasses on the hem of his shirt. "Soccer's a thinking man's game. It's kind of like chess, only more physical. You plan your moves and then you execute."

"Can you teach us some more moves?" Topher asked. Dark, curly hair hung down over eager brown eyes. Sometimes Paul thought Topher looked like a poodle who always needed a haircut.

Paul threw his math text into his locker with a bang and pulled out his earth sciences book.

"Sure," Paul said. It was kind of nice having his brainiac friends respect him for his athletic abilities, as well as his academic achievements.

Early Saturday morning their dad took Paul and Andy to another park league soccer practice. There were only two more practices before the Cedar Brook Saints' first game. Without speaking, the twins pulled their gear out of the back of the minivan.

At least once the matches started, Paul thought, *I won't have to worry about staying clear of Andy. He'll get all the playing time, while I sit on the bench.*

In the fullback position, Andy would be on the field most of the time, guarding his team's goal.

Andy left Paul at the van and headed over to Crash and Tim. When Paul walked by, he heard Andy describing the Manchester-Liverpool match.

"You guys should have seen how McCleod's cleat went right into that guy's head," Andy said. "There was blood everywhere."

Andy didn't care who heard him, Paul realized, as his brother's voice carried across the field. Paul shivered. How could they be so different from one another! He knew Andy would love to play the rough kind of soccer they'd watched on TV. Paul was afraid Andy might do something on the field, and someone would get hurt. Just then a tap on his shoulder startled Paul, and he jumped. It was Coach Benedict.

"Stewart!"

"Yes, Sir?" Paul replied.

"I got a call last night from a friend of mine, Coach Taylor over at your school," Coach Benedict said. "He told me you were an excellent forward and even beat your own brother in a game last week."

"Yeah, I guess you could say that," Paul said.

"Well, let's see some of that today, and maybe I'll start you in next week's game."

Yes!!! At last he had a chance to show what he could do.

"Thanks Coach," Paul said.

Coach Benedict blew his whistle and his players gathered around him, eager to start practice. Coach called out names and divided them up into two groups of forwards and fullbacks. They took up positions in one third of the field to work on their goal tactics.

The big guys—Andy, Tim, and Crash—took on defensive stances in front of the goal. Two others positioned themselves just at the midfield line. The coach placed Paul, Mitch, and another guy as offensive players at midfield and reminded them to move the ball into the attacking third of the field.

When Coach Benedict dropped the ball at Paul's feet, Mitch ran ahead of him and turned to meet his pass. Paul jogged steadily forward, juggling the ball back and forth between his feet, as he approached the attacking third of the field. Moving into the attack zone, Paul watched his brother and Crash rushing toward him from either side. He carefully kicked the ball with his right foot to Mitch, a forward on his left. The ball shot right to Mitch, but Andy kept rushing and slammed into Paul, knocking him down.

"What're you doing, Moron?" Paul yelled at his brother. "You knew the ball was already gone!"

"Lighten up," Andy said. "Just messin' around."

"Well, quit messing around at my expense." Paul pushed himself up off the ground and brushed the dirt and grass off his uniform. Coach signaled for the boys to take their places again.

"Watch it, Andy," Coach Benedict said. "That could have easily been a yellow card."

But Paul didn't think Coach seemed all that concerned. It was a good practice, even though Andy knocked into Paul several more times, usually when the ball wasn't even anywhere near him. Somehow, Paul kept his temper under control.

But he kept checking his watch every few minutes. His youth group was going bowling that afternoon, and he was missing out on the beginning because of practice. He wondered if Rachel would be there.

"See you later, Mom," Paul shouted as he shut the passenger door and waved goodbye. He hustled toward the double glass doors of Super Bowl, Cedar Brook's only bowling alley, where his youth group had already started their games.

He walked into the building and waited a moment as his eyes adjusted to the dim light. Finally, he saw that most of the kids from youth group had staked out lanes eight, nine, and ten.

After renting a pair of really ugly red and black bowling shoes, Paul hopped down three steps to the heavily waxed bowling lanes. He knew the shoes would be too big, since they didn't come in half sizes, so he'd brought along an extra pair of socks to wear.

Although Paul enjoyed hanging out with Gavin and the others at school, he felt most comfortable around the kids from his youth group. Here he wasn't "Andy's brother," or "the smart kid." He was just Paul.

Since everyone was already in the middle of their games, Paul didn't know quite where to land. Since Rachel was bowling on lane ten, he headed her way, hoping they had enough room for an extra player.

"Hey, Paul!" Rachel's younger sister Lisa called out. "We need an extra bowler on lane eight to even things out. Come and join us!"

Paul realized he couldn't refuse without looking dumb, so he turned back toward lane eight. It wasn't that Lisa was so bad. She was a nice girl, really. She was a year younger than Rachel, but taller. She reminded Paul of a wobbly baby giraffe, with her long neck and legs, and fawn-colored hair.

"I'm glad you're here," she said. Paul sat down on the molded plastic bench to put on his bowling shoes. "Are you any good at this?"

"At putting on shoes?" he asked with a smile. "Yeah, I've had some practice."

"No," she giggled. "I meant bowling. I haven't knocked down a single pin yet."

"I'm no expert, but I'm no slouch, either," Paul said. "Show me what you've got."

"Promise you won't laugh?" she asked.

Paul smiled and nodded. "I promise."

Lisa carefully stuck her fingers in a ball and swung it up to her chin. She took a few steps toward the line, pulled her arm back, and let the ball go. It thudded on the polished wood floor and rolled backwards.

"Okay," Paul said. "First rule of bowling. Never dribble a bowling ball."

"I *knew* you'd laugh at me," she said in frustration.

"I'm not laughing, really," he said. "I think I can help you." He grunted as he picked up her twelve-pound ball from the floor. "I know the first thing you could do—try a lighter ball."

"Just because I'm not as athletic as you, you think I can't handle a heavy ball?" she asked, folding her arms across her chest.

Paul was surprised at how defensive she sounded all of a sudden. "Hey, I don't even use a twelve-pound ball," he said. "I use a ten-pounder, which would be fine for you, but why don't you use an eight-pound ball until you get a little more control."

Together, Paul and Lisa hunted for a lighter ball, while everyone else took their turn on the lane. By the time they found one, it was her turn again.

"Now," he said. "Try looking at the arrows on the floor instead of the pins. Aim for the one just to the right or left side of the middle pin. Got it?"

Lisa nodded. She took a few steps, pulled the ball back, pushed it forward, and then released it. This time, it rolled down the middle of the lane and knocked down all but two of the pins.

"A seven-ten split!" Paul said. Her teammates clapped.

"Good going!" another girl said.

"Is that good?" Lisa asked.

"Compared to your last throw, it's great!" said Paul.

"So what do I do now?" she asked.

Paul showed Lisa that if she aimed to the far side, she could knock one of the pins toward the other one across the lane. "It's tough," he said, "but possible."

Lisa again took her place on deck and concentrated. She threw the ball and it headed for the pin on the right—the number ten pin. Paul held his breath. Her ball hit the pin, knocking it straight back. The seven pin was left standing.

"I'm such a loser," Lisa said as the pins were reset for the next bowler.

"Hey, you gave it a try. It was a tough shot," Paul said. "Some pros can't even make that."

Paul was up next. He bowled a spare. While the other people in their lane took their turns, Lisa turned to Paul and said, "Thanks, Paul. I know it's just a game, but I hate looking stupid out there. Especially…"

Her voice trailed off, and she pointed a few lanes over to where Rachel was ready to bowl. Rachel walked gracefully up to the line, released the ball, and knocked down every pin."

"See what I mean?" Lisa asked.

Paul glanced up to the electronic scoreboard hanging over Rachel and noticed that it was her third strike that game. She waved at him, and Paul waved back.

"Wow," he said.

"Yeah, try having her for a sister."

"What do you mean?" Paul asked.

"You wouldn't understand."

They both sat on the bench, waiting their turns.

"Try me."

"Do you have any idea what it's like to have a sister who's perfect? She's pretty, she's smart, *and* she's good at sports. Even bowling, which we do once a year."

"Come on," Paul said. "It can't be that bad."

"See," she said. "I knew you wouldn't understand."

Paul started to protest, but it was his turn. He bowled a split, and only picked up two pins on his second ball. When Lisa's turn came around, this time she bowled a spare. Surprised by how proud he felt of her, Paul prepared for his turn, paying more attention to his stance. Strike! Without meaning to, he glanced down the lanes to see if Rachel had seen him. She was looking right at him and smiled.

"Great shot, Paul," their youth leader Will said from the next lane. "That was great how you arced the ball so it hit that ten pin just the right way."

"Thanks, Will!"

Paul plopped down on the plastic bench and paid

more attention to his game. When it was over, Paul was surprised to see that he had bowled a one-twenty.

"I'm going to get a Coke," he said to Lisa. "You want anything?"

"Lemonade, please," she said, smiling.

On his way to the snack bar, he saw Rachel walking toward him.

"Great game," she said. "I saw your score on the overhead. You must really know what you're doing."

He wished he had some great story about how he'd been bowling since he was two, but he didn't.

"Thanks, but it was mostly just luck. And geometry. And a little quantum physics."

"At least it's not brain surgery," she said, smiling.

Paul had always liked Rachel. At least she recognized a joke when she heard it, unlike some of the other girls in the youth group.

"I guess I'll see you later," she said. "I need to get back to my game. It's too bad you're all the way down on lane eight. I was hoping we could hang out."

Rachel walked away, but Paul stood as if glued to the floor. He couldn't believe it! Rachel wanted to hang out with him? Why had he gotten stuck with Lisa?

At the end of the two games, the youth group moved over to the snack bar for pizza. Unlike most bowling alleys, Super Bowl actually served a decent slice. Paul looked around, took a deep breath, and sat in the empty seat next to Rachel.

"Hey," she said, and smiled a little bashfully.

The snack bar manager carried the pizzas out, but before they ate, Will thanked God for the food, for the time together, and for bowling shoes.

When the prayer was over, Paul asked, "Why bowling shoes?"

"Bowling shoes," Will said, "are the great equalizer. You can be the coolest kid ever, or the biggest nerd in school, but put on a pair of bowling shoes, and you look as stupid as everyone else."

"And that's a good thing?" Paul asked.

"Sure," Will said. "It's like how God looks at all of us. He knows how messed up we all are, even if we can't see it. Fortunately, he loves us anyway—bowling shoes and all."

Everyone laughed, and Paul and Rachel ate in silence for a few minutes. Paul really wanted to say something, but for the first time in his life he couldn't think of anything.

Finally, Rachel said, "So, you got to bowl with Lisa."

"Yeah," Paul said. "She was a little rough at first, but she got better."

"What do you mean?" Rachel asked, looking concerned.

"Nothing," Paul said, startled by the emotion in Rachel's voice. "She just kept bowling gutters, but with a few pointers, she got much better."

"All that quantum physics?" shel asked with a grin.

"No, she was an especially tough case. It took microbiology."

Rachel laughed. "I'm sorry, it's just that sometimes Lisa can come off as a little…harsh."

"Really?" Paul asked. "What do you mean?"

"Maybe she's just that way with me. It's like I can't do anything right. I know she thinks I'm really stupid. She's always calling me a moron. No one should ever call you that."

"Yeah, you're right," Paul said. He was glad she didn't know how many times he'd called Andy a moron.

"Thanks." Rachel looked down at her pepperoni pizza and then over at him. "I'm sorry I brought it up. I think Lisa's a really sweet girl to everyone but me."

Paul decided to change the subject. "So, who do you like better, Batman or Spiderman?"

"Spiderman, definitely," she said. "I mean, does Batman have any actual superpowers? Isn't he just a guy in a weird suit with lots of expensive toys and a dark side?"

"Absolutely," Paul said.

Forty-five minutes later, Paul's mom picked him up in front of Super Bowl.

"What are you grinning about?" she asked as he got in the minivan.

"Who's grinning?" he said, but he still couldn't stop smiling. He'd had a great time with Rachel.

When they pulled into the driveway, Paul saw Andy in the backyard kicking the soccer ball into a net he had set up as a goal. Paul thought about what Rachel had said about Lisa. Maybe he was a little hard on Andy. Besides, they would both play better soccer if they could get along. As Paul walked out to the backyard, Andy kicked the ball toward him. Paul jumped and caught it between his ankles, twisted a bit, and then kicked the ball into the net.

"So," Paul said, "did you ever think that if you spent more time trying to work with me as a teammate, and less time trying to hurt me and make me look stupid, we might actually make some great plays?"

Andy paused for a moment and sneered. "Nope, never thought of that, Doofus."

"Yeah," Paul said. "I should never have given you credit for thinking." Paul opened the backdoor and stormed inside, slamming it behind him.

Even though it was April, a winter freeze dominated the Stewart brothers' relationship. Andy and Paul barely spoke to each other, except to grunt when they passed one another in the hallway. It was no different at school. They avoided each other as much as possible.

On Thursday afternoon, Paul stayed after school for a Spanish club meeting to help Señora Granger plan a "fiesta" booth at the upcoming Around the World school fair. Since Mom wasn't picking them up until after Paul's meeting, Andy waited for Paul outside.

Ignoring most of what Señora Granger said, Paul watched his brother out the second story window playing soccer with Jimmy Hong and a couple of the other guys. Paul remembered how, not too long ago, he and Andy always kicked the ball around together while they waited for their ride home.

"Would you do that for us, Señor Stewart?" Señora Granger asked with a painfully bad Spanish accent.

"Um, yeah, definitely," Paul said. He had no idea what she had asked him.

"Bueno, bueno," she said. "I'm so glad you're willing to wear our giant sombrero around school the day of the fair to let everyone know about our fiesta."

Paul could barely contain his groan. *That's what I get for not paying attention!* But the prospect of watching Andy kick the ball around pulled Paul's interest back toward the window. This time Andy saw Paul watching him. Paul quickly looked away.

Crash! The window next to Paul rattled. Paul and the other members of the Spanish Club leaped to their feet and rushed to the windows. Standing in the courtyard, Andy and Jimmy were laughing and Andy bowed. Evidently, Andy was the one who had kicked the ball at the window with impressive precision.

Señora Granger shook her finger at the two boys, and they pretended to look apologetic, but Paul knew it was no accident. If Andy had broken the window, he would have been in big trouble.

After Spanish Club, Paul walked out to wait for his mom in the front of the school. Andy dashed around the corner just as their mom pulled up.

"Out of my way, short stuff," Andy said, running for the front seat as usual. Paul just looked at his brother with contempt and opened the back door without a fight. Andy actually hesitated as he climbed into the minivan, unsure of Paul's new attitude.

"How was your day, boys?" Mom asked as she pulled away from Cedar Brook Middle School. Both boys simultaneously grunted, "Okay."

"Paul, how was your meeting?"

"Fine," he answered, biting his tongue because he wanted so bad to tell her of Andy's stunt. "We're planning our fiesta for the fair. I'm supposed to bring supplies for *sopapillas*. Is that okay?"

"Sure, as long as you tell me what goes in a *sopapilla*," she said. "They're delicious, but I have no idea where I'd find a recipe."

"No problemo, mi madre," Paul answered. He decided not to mention anything about the sombrero. Maybe he could pull it low over his face on the day of the fair and nobody would recognize him.

"And how was your day, Andy?" Mom asked.

"Great! Crash and I kicked the ball around after school. I made some pretty good shots."

Paul glanced up at the rearview mirror and saw Andy staring at him. He knew Andy was just daring him to squeal about kicking the ball against the window. But Paul decided to keep his mouth shut.

"I've got a ton of homework," Paul told his mom. "Call me when dinner's ready, okay?"

Paul went straight to their room, knowing Andy wouldn't. Andy never did his homework right after school. The first thing he did when he walked in the house was turn on the TV and flop down on the sofa.

Paul pulled his homework out of his backpack and sat down at his desk. Soon, as he concentrated on the study questions about Hammurabi and the first code of laws he'd been assigned in world history, Paul was able to forget the feud with his brother.

After a quiet dinner, Paul asked if he could use Dad's computer in the office. "I just need to look up some stuff for school."

"Sure," Dad said. "Just don't mess with any of the paperwork on my desk."

"I won't."

"Andy, you need to get started on your homework."

"Nothing's due till Friday," Andy said.

"You need to get started early, so you'll have plenty of time to finish," Mom said.

Andy growled, "All right," and dragged himself away from the table.

Once he was out of earshot, Mom said, "Paulie, you shouldn't bury yourself in homework like this. Is it too much? Would you like me to talk to your teachers?"

"No, Mom, really. It's okay. I just have one more thing to do." He knew his mom thought he meant homework. But he had another project in mind.

Sitting at Dad's computer, Paul surfed the Internet for soccer sites that would help him improve his game.

Andy's kick that afternoon had really surprised him, and not just because it made him jump. Paul had convinced himself that he could outsmart Andy at soccer, but Andy was more than just a strong, fast runner. He could kick a ball with force and accuracy. Paul needed to work even harder on his skills.

On a couple of Internet sites Paul found actual game segments that he could watch, and he replayed them over and over. He even made notes, but finally, his hand started cramping. He rubbed the sore muscles and shut down the computer.

That's when he glanced out the window into the backyard and saw the tree house. Paul remembered how excited he and Andy were on their seventh birthday when their parents first told them they had a special gift. The brothers were told to close their eyes, and then Mom and Dad led them into the backyard.

Paul let his mind drift back to a happier time.

"Surprise!" their parents shouted.

The boys uncovered their eyes and stared at the giant oak tree in the far corner of the yard.

"It's a tree," Andy said, sounding disappointed.

Paul elbowed him and pointed to the tree house.

"Wow!" Andy shouted. "Can we play in it?"

"That's why I built it," Dad said, grinning.

The tree house was amazing. A safety railing

enclosed the deck that wrapped all the way around the giant oak and surrounded an enclosed room with a door and roof. A rope ladder was attached to a hole in the floor of the platform and could be raised to keep out invaders and lowered to bring up friends and allies. Grandpa had added a bucket on a pulley so Paul and Andy could haul up cargo and cookies.

Paul smiled in remembrance. For three years, their tree house served as a jungle fort, a pirate ship, the deck of a star cruiser, and a military outpost. Mom would have to coax them down every night just to eat dinner. A few times during the summer, they'd even been allowed to sleep in it.

Why can't Andy and I be like we were then? Suddenly, Paul realized how sad he was and how much he missed being Andy's best friend. What had changed? Why had Andy become such a jerk?

That's when another memory bubbled to the surface of Paul's mind. He remembered that at the first of sixth grade, their teacher had broken their class into two different reading and math groups. Paul was in the highest level of both groups.

One day he happened to walk by his teacher's desk and saw that she had left her grade book open. He shouldn't have looked, but he did. Paul quickly found his name and compared his grades to everyone else's. He had the highest scores in class!

Since Mom had left two days before for her once-a-year getaway with her mom and sisters, Dad had picked up Paul and Andy from school that day. Paul got in the front seat. Andy slid into the back. Paul noticed Andy handing their dad a piece of folded paper.

"Dad!" Paul said, as soon as he got in the car. "Guess what? I'm in the top group for both reading and math!"

Paul wanted his dad to be really excited. Instead, he just said, "That's nice." Then Dad looked at Andy in the rearview mirror. "How about you, Sport? How was your day?"

"Fine," Andy said. "I guess."

"Come on, tell me something good that happened," his dad pushed.

"Well, I got the fastest time on our sprints in gym class," Andy said.

"That's fantastic! I'm proud of you, Son."

Paul couldn't believe it. He was number one in his reading and math groups, and his dad didn't even care. But Andy set the fastest time on some stupid race, and Dad was thrilled.

"Hey, Andy," Paul said. "What reading group are you in?"

"Shut up, Paula," Andy said.

"That's enough, Paul," their dad said.

Paul didn't get it. He'd just asked a question. But

that night Paul saw the paper Andy had handed their dad in the car. He hadn't meant to snoop, but he was using Dad's computer, and it was just lying there on top of the desk. Andy had been placed into the lowest reading group, and their teacher was suggesting a parent-teacher conference to discuss Andy's problem.

Paul realized it was just about that time that Andy had turned into a real jerk. Paul had always thought it was because Andy was so strong he just enjoyed making Paul look weak. But now he wondered if Andy just felt bad about not being smart and had decided to take it out on Paul.

His youth pastor's voice popped into his head. "Whenever something's not going right in your life, pray about it," Will always said. "God will give you an answer." So Paul bowed his head.

Lord, I don't know what Andy's problem is. All I know is that he doesn't respect me for who I am. Please give him some sense so he'll treat me like a brother again. And Lord, give me patience so I can tolerate more of his garbage and make me the better person. In Jesus' name, Amen.

Even though he had prayed, Paul still felt sick inside, and he couldn't stop thinking about his brother.

CHAPTER:04

After school on Friday, Jimmy "Crash" Hong and Tim Howard came home with Andy to play soccer in the back yard. The first game of the season was on Sunday, and they all wanted more practice.

While Andy was out of the house, Paul went to their room and pulled out a couple of books on soccer strategy. He laid across his bed and studied the color photos of pro players. Part of him really wanted to be out there kicking the ball around with Andy and the guys. But he knew what Andy would say if he stepped foot in the backyard. Plus Paul couldn't stand being around Crash and Tim. They were worse jerks than Andy. No, Paul would depend on strategy.

When Saturday morning practice rolled around, Paul worried that Coach Benedict would make it even harder than usual. To his surprise and relief, they played a real soccer game instead of running all those miserable drills.

During practice Paul made a few nice plays and managed to stay out of Andy's way. Without Paul to rough up, Andy seemed to grow more impatient. At one point, when Andy knocked down Mitch Berry, the coach came down on him pretty hard.

"Stewart," Coach Benedict yelled. "What are you doing? We're getting ready for a game! We don't need you injuring your own teammates."

The way Coach said it, Paul wondered if he would be so upset if Andy hurt a player on *another* team. Paul glanced over at Andy, who actually looked embarrassed by the coach's reprimand.

Paul almost felt sorry for his brother. The truth was, Andy was the most aggressive player on their team, but he was also the most dedicated and the most effective. He loved soccer, and he wanted to win. And Paul recognized this, even if the Coach didn't.

"I was just trying to do my best to block the offense, Coach," Andy said, defensively.

"Save it for the game," Coach Benedict said.

The rest of the practice went better. Paul used some of the techniques he had read about in his soccer books, and they worked. He scored three points.

After practice, Coach pulled Paul aside.

"I'm going to start you tomorrow," he said.

"No kidding?" Paul was thrilled. He was excited to be playing, but even more excited that he had proven that Andy wasn't the only soccer player in the family.

"You've earned it Stewart. Your brother will be out there too."

"Thanks, Coach!"

It was no surprise that Andy would start, but Paul wasn't sure Coach would ever recognize his abilities.

After practice, the Stewarts piled into the minivan and headed for Taco Casa for lunch.

"Hey, Dad," Paul said. "Guess what? Coach says he's starting me in the game tomorrow!"

"That's great, Paul," Dad said.

"Terrific," said Mom.

Paul looked over at Andy, and his brother was actually smiling. Amazing! But Andy's smile disappeared the moment Andy knew Paul was looking at him.

"Good practice, Paulie," Andy said quietly.

Paul wanted to say something back, but he was to stunned to speak. Were he and his brother actually getting along?

Once they had received their order, Dad asked, "So who do you play tomorrow?"

"The Westmont Warriors," Andy said. He wiped some red hot sauce off his chin with a paper napkin.

"Aren't they the team that got suspended for a few games last year because some of the parents got into a fight with the ref?"

"Yep," Andy said with a mouthful of food.

"I just don't understand why some parents get so worked up over a game," Mom said.

"Actually, Mom," Paul said. "I'm less worried about the parents than the other players. I've heard they play dirty. Lots of yellow and red cards."

"There's nothing wrong with really going after it on the field," Andy said. "But they'd better know we're bringing our best game, too."

Paul frowned. He just hoped Andy watched himself and didn't hurt another player.

The next morning Andy complained about having to go to church.

"Mom! I need my sleep. I gotta be rested for the game," he said, burying his head under the pillow.

"That's no excuse," Mom said. She pulled the comforter off his bed, and Paul turned around so she wouldn't catch him laughing. "Get up and get dressed. We're leaving in a half hour."

That morning Pastor Jamison's sermon was about the humility of Jesus. He told about how Jesus had washed his disciples' feet on the night of the Last Supper. He described how Jesus had died in what was considered the most shameful way possible.

"Even though Jesus was perfect," the pastor said, "he never tried to make himself feel better by making those around him look bad."

Paul wondered if that's what Andy had been doing to him, making him look bad so Andy could feel better. But what, Paul wondered, did Andy have to feel bad about? He was popular and great at soccer.

The Stewart family had sat on the back pew this morning, and just as soon as the service was over at noon, they hurried to the parking lot. It was always a race to make game time at one o'clock. That's why so many kids on the team didn't go to church. Andy and Paul were both out of the car and racing into the house to change into their uniforms before their dad had even put the car in park.

As Paul changed into his uniform, his nerves kicked in. He hadn't played in an actual soccer game for more than two years. And today he was starting. What if he wasn't as good as he thought he was? What if he failed the coach and his team?

Paul let out his breath, and Andy looked up from pulling on his shin guards.

"Hey, Paul," he said. "You're gonna do fine. It'll be a great game."

"Thanks," Paul said, surprised, but pleased.

Andy seemed so calm and confident. Paul thought about how hard Andy practiced and how much soccer meant to him.

"You're going to have a great game too," Paul said.

"I know." But Andy said it with a smile on his face.

Dressed and ready, both brothers barreled out the front door and into the van.

At the Westmont Park district field, Coach Benedict gathered the Cedar Brook Saints around him.

"Guys, let's play a clean game. We'll show the Warriors that we're good players in every sense of the word."

Paul was relieved. He thought Coach might encourage them to play rough. He nodded his head with the other boys, showing that he understood.

The town of Westmont took its soccer seriously. The park district provided an announcer and even had an electronic scoreboard. The stands were filled with cheering fans.

With the match ready to start, Paul felt his mouth had turned to cotton it was so dry. His hands shook. Was he really ready for this? The whistle blew, signaling the start of the first period, and ready or not, Paul ran onto the field.

The players took their positions. Within seconds, the ball was in motion. Paul eyed the ball like a hawk as it was kicked to him. Behind it ran a brute of a kid in the yellow and black colors of the Warriors. But Paul knew he could handle it. He intercepted the ball and kicked it downfield away from the charging midfielder. He knew Busch and Berry were moving with him to get the ball to the defending goal.

As they reached the defensive third of the field, all

of the Warriors' players closed in on the Cedar Brook Saints. Paul delivered a side kick to the ball, sending it over to the unguarded and waiting Jeff Busch, who kicked it right into the net. Score!

Paul's nerves were shot. He glanced over at Coach Benedict, who looked stern and focused, but pleased. The Warriors' coach screamed instructions—and insults—at his players.

"Come on, McCormick, get in there and fight! Taylor, don't be such a wimp!"

For the first time, Paul decided he really liked Coach Benedict. At least he didn't scream at them.

With the ball now in the possession of the Warriors, Coach Benedict called out to Andy to defend the goal. Andy took the position of stopper, like a goalie in front of the real goalie. As the Warriors' attacker charged toward the goal, Andy didn't wait. He charged the opposing player and side-kicked, striking the player's shin and knocking him down. Pain marked the young Warriors' face. Even as the opposing player still lay on the field, Andy kicked the ball away.

Boos erupted from the Warrior fans, and the Saints side fell silent. The referee blew the whistle to stop the game and ran onto the field. The Warriors' coach and Coach Benedict charged onto the field as well.

"You'd better control your players, Benedict," the Warriors' coach yelled.

"Before you scream at me, Tucker," Coach Benedict said, "I suggest you check on your injured player."

Coach Tucker turned around angrily and stomped across the field to where his player still lay, holding his shin tightly. Paul watched as Andy went back to check on the hurt player. The Warriors coach saw him, and Paul thought it looked like the opposing coach was about to explode.

"It was an accident, sir," Andy said.

"I don't want to hear it! Ref, this deserves a call of intentional obstruction!"

"Tucker, you can't call that intentional obstruction," Coach Benedict said. "He was just trying to steal the ball. He didn't use his body to stop your kid from making the play."

But Coach Benedict's argument didn't change the outcome. The referee held up a yellow card in the air. Andy was officially cited and told any additional penalties would result in him being removed from the game.

"That's okay, Stewart," Coach Benedict said to Andy. "Looks like there's a little home field advantage here." He glared at the back of the Warriors' coach as the injured player limped off the field. The home team fans cheered loudly.

One look at Andy's face, and Paul knew his brother was furious about the call. For once, Paul didn't blame him. Paul just hoped Andy wouldn't do anything stupid.

The ref announced that the Warriors would receive a free kick from the spot of the incident. A Warriors' replacement forward took his position, and at the whistle, moved to kick the ball. The kicker sent the ball straight to the Saints' goalie, Derek Webster. He caught it. Swinging it over his head, he threw the ball to Jimmy Hong who moved forward with Andy and passed the ball to Mitch, the forward.

Mitch intercepted the ball and kicked it down to the defending goal area, where Paul was waiting to take it in. With impressive accuracy, Mitch kicked across the goal area to Paul's waiting foot. Paul pivoted and drove the ball into the net—another point for the Saints. Their fans rose and cheered, including Paul's mom and dad. Paul looked over at Andy, who winked at him, then turned to high-five Jimmy Hong. Mitch and Jeff slapped Paul on the back. Finally, Paul felt like part of the team.

Despite the Saints' early lead, the two teams were evenly matched, and the game was close. With twenty seconds left on the clock, the Saints were up 5 to 4, and the Warriors had possession of the ball. The entire Warrior team, except the goalie, charged the Saints' goal, as the Saints prepared to defend it. The Warriors' forward made a straight kick toward their goalie Derek, but it was low enough that he kicked it away. His intention was to kick it over the attacking line's heads and to his own forwards waiting at midfield. But he caught his foot on the turf and instead kicked it off the field into the Warriors' bleachers.

If the ball had hit a Saints' fan, it wouldn't have been a problem. But the ball hit a Warriors fan squarely in her chest, knocking a cup of coffee into her lap. The Warriors fans went crazy, yelling angrily at the Saints players and fans.

In the confusion, the game clock ran out. The Saints had won the game. The Warriors were furious. Many of their fans were so busy screaming at Derek and the refs that they didn't even seem to realize that the game was over. They looked over at the woman covered in coffee, jumping up and down and shaking her fist at the other side of the field. Coach Benedict's eyes met Andy and Jimmie's, and they all laughed.

When things calmed down a little, Coach Benedict gathered his team to shake hands with the Warriors. But the Warriors' coach walked his players off the field without stopping to greet or even acknowledge the waiting Saints.

"Talk about sore losers," Jimmy said.

"Guys, you played a great game," Coach Benedict said, as the team gathered around him. "I'm really proud of you. That was a great ending play, Derek."

"Derek, Derek, Derek," the team chanted.

Paul looked at Andy huddled across from him.

Andy grinned. *Maybe things have changed*, he thought. *Andy and I are actually getting along.*

"Don't let this victory go to your heads, team. We've still got a long season ahead of us. But I'm proud of you. Especially you, Stewart," Coach Benedict said, looking at Paul.

Paul was shocked. "Thanks," he said. But this time when he looked at Andy, Andy wasn't smiling.

Mom and Dad waited for them outside their van.

"Great game, guys." Dad said, hugging them at the same time.

"I'm glad you won, boys," said Mom. "It's just too bad things had to get so ugly. What happened with you and the other player, Andy?"

"It wasn't on purpose, Mom!" Andy said, defensively. "And the ref had no right to give me a yellow card."

"I think Mom just hates to see anyone get hurt," Paul said.

"If you don't shut up," Andy whispered, "you're the one who's going to get hurt."

Then Paul realized that nothing had changed. It didn't matter that they'd just worked together and played a great game of soccer. They weren't friends, and they never would be.

CHAPTER:05

The next day at school, the only topic of conversation was the Saints' win over the Westmont Warriors and the trouble that plagued the match.

"Was Andy really thrown out of the game?" a guy asked Paul in his second-period class.

"Did you really send a woman to the hospital with third-degree burns?" a sixth-grader asked Derek.

But the biggest news from the game was what a great soccer player Paul Stewart turned out to be. The gym class victory, the school learned, was not a fluke. One rumor was that Paul had scored twelve goals, two of them after he sprained an ankle.

The win in gym class had gained Paul some respect from Gavin, Topher, and Stephen, but now the whole school was talking. Suddenly, Paul was the center of attention. Kids who he thought didn't even know his name patted him on the back and congratulated him. Girls actually noticed him and smiled. He felt a little strange about it, especially since most of the stuff people were saying wasn't true. But he'd never had that kind of attention before, and he kind of liked it.

The only person who completely ignored him was Andy. It made Paul nervous. As he crossed the cafeteria to eat with Gavin, he waited for his brother to trip him, throw food at him, or call him a loser. Nothing. Nada. Zip.

"You and Cro-Magnon Man getting along better now?" Gavin asked, nodding toward Andy.

"If you mean are his grunts less hostile than usual, yeah," Paul answered, but he had to admit deep down inside that he was a little worried about Andy.

At practice the next Saturday, Coach gathered his players together for an assessment of the game.

"You know, guys," Coach Benedict began. "One of your parents called me last Sunday. At first I didn't want to hear any of it, but the more I listened, I realized he was right. We have a good team, and we deserved to win that game. And the Warriors and their fans behaved like jerks. But I shouldn't have laughed when that woman got splashed with coffee. Their bad behavior doesn't make our's okay.

"I want us to be careful. Many of you are quick, strong players. That's great. But we shouldn't use our strength alone to win. If we do, we'll wind up with more red cards than victories. We need to rely more on strategy and teamwork and less on aggressive playing."

Coach looked directly at Jimmy and Andy.

"Paul," he continued, "is a great example of the kind of playing I mean. We couldn't have won that game last week without him. And he did it without any roughness."

Paul didn't want to be a jerk, so he tried to hide the smile that threatened to stretch across his face.

"We're a strong team, guys. Let's show the other teams we can win fair and square. We have another game against the Warriors next month. They'll be out for blood because we beat them, but we need to take them on with level heads and great playing. Okay?"

"Okay, Coach," they all said in unison.

"Good. That's behind us. Let's practice for the next match."

Andy walked up behind Paul while Coach Benedict worked one-on-one with Derek.

"Dad was the one who called, wasn't he?" Andy asked. "Did you put him up to it?"

Paul looked at his brother and shrugged. He didn't know for sure, but he suspected it was Dad who had called. It was something he would do.

"Now everyone loves you, don't they, Paulie?" Andy said. "Paulie's just the greatest. You know what, Paul? You're not fooling me. I know you play smart because you're too weak to play any other way."

"Shut up, Andy," Paul said.

"You shut up!"

"Wow, that was a great comeback," Paul said. "Did you have to stay up all night to think up that one?"

"Why'd you ever start playing soccer again?" Andy walked away without waiting for an answer.

During practice, Paul noticed Coach watching them closely. Whenever Andy got near another player, Coach would say something like, "Stewart, concentrate on the game, not on knocking people over."

Andy totally avoided Paul. His brother even missed a few balls Paul passed to him. It was like he refused to even acknowledge Paul existed. Paul couldn't decide which was worse: Andy yelling at him and punching him in the arm, or pretending he wasn't even there.

After practice the family headed for Taco Casa again. Paul now dreaded the weekly tradition. Spending quality family time together had lost all of its appeal.

"Did you have a bad practice, Andy?" Mom asked.

"It was okay," Andy said. "Why?"

"You just don't seem very happy today."

"The coach is totally changing things around," Andy said. "He never used to have a problem with the way I played. Today he came down on me really hard about everything."

"Maybe he's just concerned about the way things went at last week's game," Mom said.

"Or maybe he's doing it because Paul is a big cry

baby," Andy said sarcastically.

"Andy, that wasn't necessary," said Mom.

"What's wrong, Son?" Dad asked.

"You called Coach, didn't you, Dad?" Andy asked.

Their dad was quiet for a moment and then said, "Yes I did. But I called him because I didn't think he set a good example for his team during the game."

"I can't believe you, Dad. Soccer is supposed to be rough. What about Manchester and Liverpool?"

"Andy, those are grown men playing professional soccer. They're not middle-schoolers in a park league."

"If you could just play more like Paul," Mom said.

Paul tried not to groan out loud. His own mother had just signed his death warrant.

"Mom, Andy's a great player just the way he is," Paul said.

"Shut up, Paul. I don't need you to defend me," Andy said.

Paul felt his own temper rising. "I'm sick of you telling me to shut up!" he yelled, attracting the attention of several other diners.

"Boys—" their mom began.

"Shut up!" Andy and Paul said at the same time.

Everything got very quiet. Paul hadn't really meant to tell Mom to shut up, and he figured Andy hadn't either. But that didn't change the fact that they were both in big-time trouble.

"Andy. Paul. Get in the van," their dad said angrily. "You're both grounded for one week."

"Yes, Sir," they both said at the same time.

Paul and Andy knew better than to argue. Silently, they picked up their trays, dumped their trash in the garbage can, and walked outside to climb into the backseat. Neither of them spoke. A few minutes later their parents slid into the front, and Dad turned around to look at them sternly.

"Don't you ever tell your mother to shut up again. Do you understand me?"

"Yes, Sir," the twins said.

"What do you have to say to your mother?"

"I'm sorry, Mom," Paul said.

"Me too," Andy echoed his brother.

For most of the ride home, there was total silence until Paul spoke up. "Dad?"

"What?" his dad said.

"I know we're grounded, but I've signed up to help out with a service project at church this afternoon. We're doing spring cleaning and yard work for some older members. I don't want to let Will down."

"You should have thought of that before you told your mother to shut up," his father said.

"Honey," their mom said. "It's a church function. They're depending on his help."

"All right," Dad said. "You can go. But after that,

you are grounded. No TV. No phone."

Groundings had never been a big deal for Paul anyway. He didn't watch much TV during the week or talk on the phone.

"Me too," Andy said. "I signed up too."

Paul knew his brother was lying. But Andy kicked him—hard—and Paul kept his mouth shut.

"Really?" their dad said. "I find that hard to believe. But I'm glad to see you getting involved. All right. A little work won't hurt you."

Paul couldn't believe it. His dad actually fell for Andy's scam. Sighing, Paul turned to look out the window at the passing scenery. After the minivan pulled into the driveway, the brothers headed straight to their room.

"Since when have you ever volunteered for anything at church?" Paul asked.

"Since it gets me out of being grounded for the afternoon," Andy said. "Even hanging out with those losers is better than being stuck here with no TV."

"You're disgusting," Paul said, flopping on his bed.

"Right back at ya," Andy said. He picked up a soccer magazine and turned his back on Paul.

At two-thirty, Mom drove the silent twins to church, where Will met them in the parking lot.

"Hi, Rachel," Paul said, sliding out of the backseat. He was glad to see her. "Lisa." Paul was going to be sure he didn't get matched up with Rachel's sister again.

"Hi, Paul." Rachel smiled warmly. Lisa just turned her back on the pair.

Rachel followed him to the back of the van, where Paul pulled out a couple of rakes and a spade. Andy stood off to the side with his hands in his pockets.

"When should I pick you boys up?" Mom asked.

"Eight o'clock," Paul said.

"That's pretty late to be working in people's yards, isn't it?"

Will walked up to the driver's side and spoke to her. "After the Spring Clean-up, we'll come back here for Groovy Movie Night."

"*Really*," Mom said, raising her eyebrows at Paul. "My sons didn't mention that to me." She paused and said, "I guess it's all right." She looked sternly at both Paul and Andy. "I'll see you at eight o'clock sharp."

"Yes, ma'am," the twins answered.

Will gathered the youth group around him to receive instructions.

"We need to break into three groups," Will said. "One group will clean the inside of Mrs. Ingram's house. She broke her hip a few months ago and can't get around except with a walker. The second group will work in her yard, raking out leaves from last fall, pulling weeds, and planting some flowers donated by Rachel's dad's nursery. Group three will be assigned to

Mrs. Huddleston's yard. She's Mrs. Ingram's neighbor. She hasn't come to church since her husband died five years ago. I think helping her out would really encourage her."

Will divided the twenty-two middle-schoolers into three groups before he noticed Andy standing off to the side.

"Hey, Andy!" Will said. "Good to see you. Come on over here and be part of group number one with me."

At first Paul was disappointed not to be in Will's group, but then he noticed that Lisa was in that group too. Rachel, on the other hand, was with him in group number three. The day was getting better and better.

Piling into three vans, the kids were driven a couple of miles away to Mrs. Ingram's neighborhood. When they arrived, Paul got out of the van and helped unload the rakes, spades, flowers, and bags of mulch. Rachel, who had worked in her dad's nursery for the last couple of years, was in charge of group number three.

"Amy and Cheyenne, why don't you rake the dead leaves and brush out from around the bushes? Then you can bag it up and take it to the curb. Paul, you and I will plant the petunias and impatiens. Kyle and Donovan, you can spread mulch around the bushes. Once we've got the flowers planted, you can spread mulch around them too. Just be sure not to get the mulch too close to the roots. Tory and Sean, maybe you can help the girls rake leaves."

Paul had never seen Rachel take charge of anything. She really knew what she was doing. And he was more than willing to help. He carried the flats of flowers to the beds next to Mrs. Huddleston's yard.

"Leave the petunias there, please, Paul," Rachel said. "I'll take these impatiens to the bed underneath the maple. They have to be planted in the shade."

Soon Rachel and Paul were busy digging and planting pink and purple petunias. Rachel showed him how to loosen the dirt around the roots once he pulled the flower out of the flat.

Working next to Rachel, Paul noticed how nice she smelled. *Like vanilla*, he thought. Then as he dug another hole, he accidentally threw some dirt at Rachel.

"I'm sorry!" he said. "Are you okay?"

"My eye! You got dirt in my eye!" Rachel cried as she covered her face with her hands.

Paul felt terrible. He scooted over to her to make sure she was okay. When he was just a few inches away from her, she lifted her head.

"Just kidding!" Then she dropped a handful of dirt in Paul's hair.

"You're not getting away with that!" Laughing, Paul threw a clump of dirt that hit Rachel in the shoulder. She threw some old mulch back at him. Soon they were in an all-out dirt fight, running and squealing around the yard.

"Ouch!" Paul said, when she got him in the back of the head.

"Don't worry, Paul," she said. "A little dirt never hurt anybody."

The two of them were laughing so hard they could barely breathe or throw their ammunition. But a moment later—

"Rachel!" It was Lisa. "What are you doing? This looks like a disaster. Do you think Mrs. Huddleston will appreciate having clumps of dirt all over her yard?"

"We'll clean it all up, Lisa," she said.

"It's my fault," Paul said. "We were just having fun."

"Honestly, Rachel," Lisa said. "You act like such a child. You'd better get back to work."

Rachel was already picking up the dirt. Paul got a broom and swept the sidewalk. They planted the rest of the flowers quickly and quietly.

Paul's perfect afternoon had been ruined. He didn't know if Rachel was mad at him, at Lisa, or at both of them. But she wasn't laughing anymore.

A few times, Paul saw Andy go in and out of Mrs. Ingram's house, usually carrying old boxes or bags of trash. He and Lisa worked together to wash the windows. Andy, being taller, washed the outside while Lisa washed the inside. They actually looked like they were having a good time together.

Paul couldn't believe Andy had managed to weasel his way out of being grounded. He knew he should be glad his brother was helping the youth group, but he thought, *Once the grounding is over, he'll never show up again.*

When the youth group had completed their work, a smiling Mrs. Ingram presented them all with little bags of chocolate-chip cookies. Paul took his and saw that she had written a Bible verse on a slip of paper and attached it with a ribbon to the bag. It read, *Dear children, let us stop just saying we love each other; let us really show it by our actions,* (1 John 3:18 NLT).

"Thank you so much for all you've done to help an old lady," Mrs. Ingram said. "You can't imagine how much I appreciate it."

"You're welcome," Will said.

"We really enjoyed ourselves," Rachel said. "It was fun helping you and Mrs. Huddleston."

Paul looked at Rachel and their grins widened.

As they said their goodbyes, waving back at the elderly lady standing in her doorway, the kids piled into the vans to return to church. Paul felt really good inside and forgot for a moment that he was grounded. Even Andy seemed to be having fun, laughing with Lisa.

Back at the church, everyone clattered down the basement stairs for Groovy Movie Night. The normally musty smell had been replaced by the aroma of fresh popcorn. Before the kids plopped into worn-out sofas, bean-bag chairs, or on giant floor pillows, they filed past the refreshment table.

"Popcorn! Get your popcorn here!" Will's fiancé, Laura, joked while she handed out white bags of popcorn.

"Take a can of pop and find a place to flop," Will said. "The movie's about to begin."

Paul looked around the room for a seat and felt a hand on his shoulder.

"Hey, Paul," Will said. "Good job with the flowers. You and Rachel seemed to have a good time."

"Sorry about the dirt fight," Paul said, a little embarrassed.

"No problem," Will said. "I thought it was hysterical."

"Lisa Cassidy didn't think so," Paul said.

"Lisa's a really hard worker. She doesn't appreciate goofing around," Will said. "I, on the other hand, am a youth pastor, which means I do."

Paul grinned. He knew how hard Will worked. Even though he was only paid for part-time work, he treated it like a full-time job.

"It's really great to see Andy here," Will continued. "How'd you convince him to come?"

"I didn't have anything to do with it," Paul said. He hated to tell Will the real reason his twin brother showed up.

"Don't be so modest, Paul," Will said. "Andy really respects you. He told me so."

"Huh? Are you sure you were talking to Andy *Stewart*?" Paul asked.

"Yes, the Andy Stewart. I hope you can bring him back. I know it must be hard on you that Andy isn't more serious about his walk with Christ. I'm sure you've been praying for him to come back for a long time."

"Yeah." The lights dimmed.

"See you after the movie, Paul," Will said and walked away.

Paul felt so guilty. It had never really occurred to him to think about Andy's relationship with Christ. It had been a relief to get away from Andy. He'd never worried about why his brother didn't come. And he sure hadn't prayed for Andy, at least not in that way. *Some Christian I am*, he thought.

Where was Andy? He looked around the darkened room and spotted him lounging in a beanbag chair next to Lisa. His red-headed twin brother actually looked like he was having a good time. Rachel sat in a chair near the back of the room, and there was a empty chair next to her's. Paul grabbed a bag of popcorn and a soda before walking over to her.

"Is this seat clean?" he asked.

"Mulch-free, I promise," she said. "Listen, I'm

sorry about being such a grouch this afternoon. I just hate it when Lisa acts all superior . . . like she's so much smarter and better than me."

"Don't let her get to you," Paul said. "I think she's just jealous."

"Jealous?" Rachel asked. "Of me? Why?"

"You know, you're popular. You're good at sports. You're, um, pretty." Paul was glad the lights were dimmed, and she couldn't see him blush.

"Thanks," she said, looking down. "But I'm not as smart as she is, and she let's me know it all the time. She just thinks she's so much better than me."

Will turned on the DVD player, and the movie credits started to roll.

"Ah, forget about her for now," Paul whispered. "Let's just have a good time." Then he threw a piece of popcorn at her.

She giggled. "Don't start that again," she whispered.

Paul was glad he had made her smile.

"Ladies and Gentlemen," Will began.

Someone yelled from the back. "I don't think there are any ladies or gentlemen here."

"I stand corrected," Will said. "Rebels and hooligans, welcome to this month's Groovy Movie. Tonight's feature film is the classic *The Parent Trap*, starring some girl, twice. Please turn off all cell phones, and refrain from throwing popcorn at the screen."

Paul had never seen the movie before. It was about two twins who had been separated at birth, but met each other at a summer camp. They were total opposites. One was smart and stuck up. The other was outdoorsy and adventurous.

At camp, the girls hated each other and played elaborate pranks to get back at the other one. When they realized they were twins and became friends, they hatched a plan to get their parents back together. Of course, by the end of the movie, that's what happened and everyone lived happily ever after.

As silly as it all was, Paul realized it was a lot like him and Andy. They spent too much of their time and energy harassing each other. When they did work together—like at the soccer match—things were great. Paul just didn't have any idea how to make that happen more often.

He thought about what Rachel had said about Lisa. He couldn't believe Rachel let Lisa bother her so much. *What if I make Andy feel the same way Lisa makes Rachel feel?* Paul wondered. *Nah! That's ridiculous. Girls are the only ones who let dumb stuff like that get to them.*

After the movie, Will gathered everyone together in a prayer circle. Paul wondered what Andy would do. His brother always said he hated the "touchy feely" stuff at church. But there Andy was, holding hands with Lisa on one side and Will on the other.

"Dear God," Will prayed, "thank you so much that we were able to help out Mrs. Ingram and Mrs. Huddleston today. We pray that by showing Mrs. Huddleston that we care, she'll see how much you care for her too. Thanks for all these kids who worked so hard today—just because they love you. Help us show your love to every person we meet because everyone is special to you. In Jesus' name we pray. Amen."

Soon Paul and Andy stood outside, waiting for Mom to pick them up. Neither one of then knew what to say to the other, but Paul had been challenged by Will's words.

"So, what did you think?" Paul asked.

"The popcorn was good," Andy said.

"That's not what I meant." Sometimes Andy really pushed his buttons.

"Do you mean, did I have a good time hanging out with your dorky friends and your weirdo youth minister?"

"Forget it," Paul said. He walked away from Andy and turned his back on him.

"Actually," Andy said. "It wasn't so bad."

That's when their mom pulled up. Andy climbed into the back seat. For Paul, life couldn't get any stranger.

CHAPTER:06

Paul and Andy were grounded for the rest of the week. Other than school, soccer practice on Saturday, and their soccer game on Sunday against the Belleville Flames, they were "confined to quarters," as Dad put it.

Part of Paul hoped that being grounded for a week would give him and Andy some time to hang out and patch things up, but part of him dreaded how Andy might reject him. But nothing happened. Andy completely ignored Paul for the most part. Paul had always hated how much Andy picked on him, but he decided that being ignored was almost worse.

On Sunday afternoon at the game, they at least managed to work together and helped lead their team to victory.

When their grounding was over, Andy started attending some youth group activities. Paul didn't tell Andy about them, so he figured Lisa Cassidy must have invited Andy. Even at youth group though, Andy ignored

Paul and spent most of his time hanging with Lisa.

One night, Andy even brought Jimmy "Crash" Hong with him. Would miracles never cease? Had the earth been knocked off its axis?

"Hey, Crash," Paul said, as he reached for a soda.

"You can call me Jimmy," he said.

"Sure," Paul said. "Whatever you say." He meant it. He didn't want to mess with Crash.

Even at school, Andy and his buddies stopped tripping Paul in the cafeteria, or bumping into him in the hall. It was weird!

When school ended in May, Paul threw himself into soccer. The Cedar Brook Saints were undefeated and in a position to capture the league championship. But they had one more match with the Westmont Warriors. Tensions were running high.

On the morning of the game, waves of heat blasted Andy and Paul as they hopped out of their parents' minivan at the soccer field parking lot. For the last week, a hot wind had blown out of the south and made June feel more like August.

"Make sure you boys drink lots of water today," Mom reminded them.

Paul knew his mom was nervous about this game with the Warriors. "Don't worry, Mom. The refs will watch this game closely. We'll be fine."

But he wasn't so sure. After they split off, Mom and Dad climbed the bleachers to sit with the other Cedar Brook fans, and Paul and Andy walked to their bench and sat down. They still weren't talking much.

"Hey, good luck," Paul said awkwardly.

"Yeah," Andy replied. "You too."

They separated and took their seats for the coach's pre-game pep talk. Paul's eyes scanned the bleachers. Even though it was a home game for the Saints, the four sets of aluminum stands were packed with Warriors fans. Some had brought lawn chairs. Most were dressed in their black and gold team colors and crowded out the handful of Saints fans who arrived in time to get the few remaining bleacher seats. The heat electrified the air. The huge crowd had been looking forward to this final match between the two teams.

Paul thought the green soccer field looked like a picture in one of his soccer magazines, freshly mown and painted. Looking up, Paul could see the main strip of downtown Cedar Brook. He wondered if the people in the diner across the street would watch the game from the comfort of air-conditioned booths.

"Okay, Saints," Coach Benedict said. "I want to see you play a good, clean game. Use the crowd's energy to help you play your best, but don't get caught up in all the rivalry. You're a smart, talented team. You can beat these Warriors without stooping to their tricks. Now, get out there and win!"

As the team broke, Paul saw Andy pull Jimmy and Tim aside and whisper something to them. Paul hoped Andy wasn't telling them to play dirty, but it was too late to do anything about that now.

The starting line up was sent to the field. Just as in the last game against the Warriors, Andy Stewart and Jimmy Hong would play the fullback positions, Derek Webster was the goalie, Mitch Berry and Paul would play as forwards, assisting the center Jeff Busch. And Tim Howard would handle midfield.

As the visiting Warriors kicked the first ball into the midfield area, the focus shifted to the match. Within the first two minutes, the Saints had scored their first goal, thanks to Mitch who drove the ball through the defending fullbacks in a breakaway play that caught the Warriors' goalie off guard. The play met with thunderous applause from the outnumbered Saints fans and jeering from the Warriors' fans. The unrelenting sun that beat down on the crowded aluminum bleachers fueled the already angry, agitated crowd.

The Warriors took possession of the ball. The Saints' goalie threw the ball toward midfield, where it was intercepted by the Warriors' midfielder. He kicked it to the forward who then cross-kicked the ball into the goal area. The Saints' goalie dove and deflected the incoming low ball. Then Derek grabbed the ball and threw it long to Tim Howard, who executed a header and passed it to Paul. As Paul prepared to drive the ball to Mitch, a defending Warriors' fullback, who had come out on the field from the sidelines, ran a shoulder charge and knocked Paul flat on his back.

Coach Benedict jumped off the bench and looked to the ref to call a foul, but the official ruling was that the defender hadn't touched the ball so it was a legal move. Paul picked himself up off the ground and resumed his place in the game, with the ball now in the Warriors' possession. Paul watched as the ball moved closer toward Andy and the goal.

Andy saw the ball coming. He had the perfect opportunity to go on the defensive with a similar contact move against the Warriors. He turned to look at Coach Benedict, hoping for approval, but the coach clearly shook his head no. Paul could tell Andy was frustrated. But Andy followed coach's orders and charged the player in a bluff that allowed Jimmy Hong to run across the field and steal the ball with no physical contact.

Jimmy then moved the ball so that he could safely pass it back to Tim in the midfield. It was the smartest way to keep the ball away from the Saints' goal. Tim received the pass and spun on his heel to kick the ball to Jeff Busch. Then Jeff passed it to Paul, who kicked it square into the Warriors' goal.

Paul jumped with excitement as soon as he knew the ball was safely in the net. Jeff and Mitch ran over to high-five him for the shot just as the ball was kicked back into the field for the Warriors' fullback to guard as it made its way to midfield.

Twenty minutes into the game, Coach Benedict sent little Marty Jenkins in to sub for Paul.

"What's up, Coach?" Paul asked when he reached the bench, breathing hard. "I was fine out there."

"You just seemed a little winded," Coach Benedict told him. "Catch your breath and save your legs—we'll need you later in the game."

Paul dropped to the bench, but he didn't like it. He hated to look weak in front of Andy. Andy ran by, looked at Paul, and then grinned at Jimmy. Paul was afraid of what the two of them were up to.

At halftime, the score was 4 to 0 in the Saints' favor. As the thermometer rose to almost ninety, the attitudes of the Warriors' fans took a nose dive. Tempers flared among the crowd.

"You guys are playing a great match," Coach Benedict told them. "You're proving that you're the superior team. Just don't quit on me. We've still got a lot of game to go, and the Warriors usually come out stronger in the second half."

The whistle blew, signaling the start of the second half. Coach Benedict put Paul back into the game.

The Warriors had possession of the ball. They drove it in from midfield all the way through to the Saints' goal before the defending fullbacks could react. A solid kick drove the ball into the Warriors' goal, pushing itself against the back net. A Warriors' fan blew an air horn, practically splitting the eardrums of those close by, and several others used noisemakers.

"Coach wasn't kidding about them having a stronger second half," Mitch said to Paul.

With the ball back to the Saints, the team shook off the Warriors' goal. Leaving Derek in as goalkeeper and Jimmy as a sweeper to defend the goal, the rest of the team formed an offensive line and charged the Warriors. As they crossed into the attacking third of the field, a Warrior fullback shoulder charged Jeff, who was leading the ball into the goal area. The player caught Jeff in the chest, knocked him over, and stole the ball. Jeff lay flat on his back, but the opposing player continued kicking the ball down field. The referee blew his whistle just as the Warriors kicked the ball from left field into the Saints' goal. As the crowd cheered, the ref signaled that the point was no good and he held up a yellow card.

Coach Benedict ran onto the field and pushed his way through to his injured player. The blow to Jeff's chest had knocked the wind out of him, and he was still gasping for breath. The coach lifted Jeff to a sitting position as one of the referees ran over to assess the situation.

"Intentional foul," the ref signaled. "Number twelve gets a yellow card. Saints will receive a free kick."

The Warriors' fans booed the referee as he turned away and walked to center field. He spoke with Coach Benedict for a moment and then called Mitch to come with him. They walked to the middle of the defending third and the ref placed the ball off center. With no Warriors' allowed in the area except for the goalie, Mitch dribbled the ball a few feet to the right then side kicked it over the goalie's head and under the top bar for a point. The outnumbered Saints' fans cheered as the Warriors' fans jeered. The score was now 5 to 1.

In a fit of anger, Coach Tucker of the Westmont Warriors threw down his clipboard. The ref pointed at the Warriors' coach and then approached him. Paul watched, getting nervous as tempers flared. The referee pointed to Coach Tucker's clipboard and then at the coach's chest. Paul couldn't hear what they were saying, but the Warriors' coach waved his arms in the air as he argued with the ref. When the ref threatened the coach with a yellow card for unsporting behavior, Coach Tucker backed down.

The Warriors were now in possession of the ball. The center jogged the ball from side to side as his forwards moved around the defending line of the

Saints. Andy waited. Suddenly, with a burst of speed, he ran across the field, knocking shoulder-to-shoulder with a forward who tried to block him. The Warriors' coach stood up in protest, but the referee pointed again for him to sit down. Andy slid sideways into the ball, knocking it away from the Warriors' center without hurting the player. But the opposing player delivered a subtle kick to Andy's ribs before Paul's twin brother could get up.

"You'll regret that, dude," Andy said as he stood up, holding his side. He ran after the ball, but fortunately, Tim had intercepted it and was moving to the Warriors' goal. Andy pulled back to stay in his defending area. Paul watched as Tim passed the ball toward Mitch, waiting for it closer to the goal. As Mitch moved to intercept the ball, the goalie ran out of the box and kicked the ball into the air away from the Warriors' goal. It sailed through the air and landed midfield just before the Saints' defending third.

The ball was now in the possession of the Warriors' forward, who had kicked Andy in the ribs. Andy ran after the opposing player, while Jimmy ran toward the forward from the opposite direction. Jimmy moved in to steal the ball, but the aggressive forward held his arm straight out to block Jimmy, hitting him squarely in the face. Jimmy fell backward and rubbed his jaw.

Andy slammed into the attacking forward, but not

before the player kicked the ball into the Saints' goal. The player fell forward into the goalpost. Rubbing his shoulder, he turned to rise and glared at Andy.

"Don't mess with me," Andy said to him as the crowd went wild over the Warriors' point. Noisemakers blared, and the air horn blew again.

The referee gave control of the ball to the Saints. As Derek prepared to kick the ball, his midfielders went into a sprint to meet it. But as his foot made contact, the man in the bleachers with the air horn sounded it again, causing Derek to fumble. He kicked the ball into the waiting Warriors' forward, who returned the kick into the net.

The referee called the score valid. Coach Benedict rose from the bench, protesting. The ref looked at him and told him to sit down. Instead, the coach called for the referee to come over.

"First you don't call it when my player gets a deliberate kick in the ribs," Coach Benedict said. "Then you fail to call against a blatant interference from the other team's fans. Come on, ref, keep it fair."

"Are you suggesting my calls aren't fair?"

"I'm suggesting you keep it fair," Coach said. The ref held up a yellow card, calling a bench foul against Coach Benedict.

"That's your warning," the ref said. "Any more accusations and you're out for the game."

Noticeably upset, Coach Benedict held his tongue and took his seat as the game resumed. Derek again went to kick the ball, but stopped as the air horn guy sounded it again. He then kicked the ball.

In the stands, tensions ran high. A few of the Saints' parents and fans were yelling at the guy blowing the air horn to knock it off. He laughed. Then the father of one of the Saints' players stood up and pushed his way over. He grabbed at the air horn, but the man holding it and the people around him pushed the player's dad back. The unruly fan aimed the air horn directly at the face of the Saints' fan, causing him to lunge forward.

"Help!" the air horn operator yelled. "I'm being attacked!"

The Warriors' fans grabbed the Saints' dad and shoved him off the bleachers just as the referee blew his whistle to stop the game.

"If this game gets any more out of control, I'm going to end it," the referee announced to the crowd.

It was the Saints' ball. Tim kicked it into the attacking third, starting the match up again. Paul received and dribbled the ball toward the goal, but once again was knocked over by a charging fullback. The fullback kicked the ball through to the midfielder who then moved it to one of his forwards in the Saints' defending third. Andy planted himself to take the charge. The Warriors' forward crashed into Andy's shoulder, knocking him off balance, and pushed Andy away. As Andy went for the ball, the referee blew the whistle.

The call was against Andy. "Intentional foul on Saints' number ten, Andy Stewart. Because I've already issued a warning, Stewart will receive a red card."

The obnoxious air horn blasted in triumph. Paul could tell Andy had been pushed past his limit. Andy planted a solid kick on the ball, shooting it straight into the bleachers and right into the man's face.

Just like that day during our Spanish Club meeting, Paul thought.

The Warriors' fans charged the field, throwing bottles, cans, food, and whatever else they could put their hands on. An angry fan picked up his unopened can of soda. Seeing Paul's jersey with "Stewart" imprinted across the back, he hurled the can at Paul's head.

Paul's head felt like it exploded in pain before everything went dark. He didn't even know when he hit the ground face first.

Andy watched in horror as Paul fell forward and sprinted toward his brother. A couple of the Warriors' players, assuming Andy wanted to fight, jumped the redhead and pounded on him. But Andy, driven by adrenaline and fear, pushed his attackers off and ran toward Paul. Several of the other Saints' players had already come to Paul's aid.

"Call 9-1-1!" Mr. Stewart shouted at his wife before

following the crowd onto the field.

The referees' whistles shrilled over and over to calm the melee, but both teams were on the field pushing and shoving each other. Dodging debris, Paul and Andy's parents pushed through the crowd. Andy crouched over Paul, protecting him from being trampled. Paul's head and face were covered in blood, mixed with grape soda. The weapon still sprayed a mist of sticky purple liquid over the field.

Mrs. Stewart cried and knelt down by her injured son as sirens wailed in the background. Finally realizing that someone was seriously hurt, the crowd backed away, making a path for the Cedar Brook Fire Department's EMT truck.

CHAPTER:07

Struggling through the dark tunnel toward the light, Paul heard distant, muffled voices. A loud buzzing noise made it hard to understand the words. As Paul slowly opened his eyes, a man's face hovered over him. He fought to move, he couldn't. His head was strapped down.

"It's okay, Son," the man said softly. "We've strapped down your head to keep you from moving. Can you hear me?"

Paul stopped struggling.

"Yes." Paul thought his voice sounded faraway.

"I'm Dr. Manning. Can you see me?"

"Yes."

"Good." The doctor opened Paul's right eye wider with the side of his thumb and shined a light into it. He did the same with the left eye. "His pupils are dilated. Very common with concussions. I'd like to get him up to X-ray right away. We'll leave him in the neck brace and strapped to the hard board until we can assess him for skull fractures. I don't want to risk more damage until we know what we're dealing with. We won't stitch up that head wound yet, either, but it's clean and we've bandaged it for now to prevent infection."

Paul wondered who the doctor was talking to. "Thanks Doc," Paul heard his Dad say. With great effort, Paul strained his eyes left to see his parents standing nearby.

"What happened? Where am I?"

"You're in the emergency room at Cedar Brook General," Dr. Manning said.

He had a nice smile, Paul thought. "My head hurts."

"Paulie, you were hit in the head with an unopened soda can at the soccer game," his mom told him.

Mom stroked his dark, straight hair back from his forehead and kissed him on the cheek. Her hand felt so good, cool to the touch like when he had a fever. His Dad took his hand.

"Where's . . . how's Andy?" Paul asked.

His parents looked at one another with concern.

"He stepped out for a minute," Dad said.

"He didn't get hurt?" Paul asked, his voice barely able to whisper through the pain.

"No, honey, he didn't," his mom reassured him.

Looking back down at Paul, Dr. Manning asked him to wiggle his toes. He did, slowly. The doctor then asked him to wiggle his fingers. Again, he succeeded.

"Very good, Paul," Dr. Manning said.

"You should see me play 'Yankee Doodle' on my armpits," Paul joked.

"Well, at least you haven't lost your sense of humor," the doctor said. "That's good!"

A young man with curly blonde hair, wearing a white lab coat, came to take Paul to X-ray.

"Promise not to run into any walls," Paul said.

"I'll do my best." The young man laughed as he pushed Paul's gurney out of the room.

"Mom?"

"We're right behind you, Son," Dad said.

After X-rays, a CT scan, and stitches, Paul finally was moved into a hospital room to spend the night. Dr. Manning had left orders that the neck brace be removed, but because of the concussion, he wanted to keep Paul in the hospital overnight for observation.

After the nursing staff made Paul as comfortable as possible, the nurse spoke to his mother.

"Paul's a very fortunate young man," she said. "No fractures or bleeding on the brain. He should be able to go home tomorrow."

The nurse smiled at Paul as she checked his I.V. fluid. "Are you hungry?"

"Starving," Paul said.

"I'll make sure they send you up some dinner in a

little while. In the meantime, would you like a can of grape soda?" The nurse's eyes twinkled.

In spite of everything, Paul grinned. "I think I'll stick with water."

After the nurse left the room, Paul asked, "Mom, please tell me what's going on with Andy."

"What do you mean, sweetheart?" she said, gently stroking his forehead.

"I can tell you don't want to talk about whatever it is, but please tell me. You're kind of scaring me."

Mom hesitated. "After you were hit," she said, "the police came. While the EMT's worked on you, the police questioned Andy. Evidently, the man with the air horn wants to press charges."

"What?!" Paul said. He tried to sit up, but he was so dizzy that he fell back on his pillow. Mom laid a calming hand on his cheek.

"It's going to be all right, honey. He claims Andy broke his nose. Anyway, the police took Andy down to the station for questioning."

"You're kidding!"

"I knew I shouldn't have told you," she said.

"Is that where Dad is now?"

"Yes, as soon as we were sure you were okay, he went down to be with Andy. I spoke with him a few minutes ago."

"And?" Paul asked.

"No charges will be filed," she said. "Evidently, it's illegal for a civilian to use an air horn within the city limits. The officer in charge is a friend of your dad's. He made it clear to the man that if he pressed charges against Andy, the police would press charges against him for inciting a riot. Not surprisingly, the guy backed down. Andy and your dad are on the way to the hospital right now."

"Great," Paul said, not sure if he meant it.

"Paul," his mother said. "Your brother feels terrible about what happened."

"Uh, huh," he said. With the pain medication in his system, Paul felt so relaxed.

"Get some rest now," his mom told him. "I'll be right here when you wake up."

Surrounded by a thick, hazy blue cloud, Paul ran down the green soccer field. He was scared. Suddenly, he heard loud noises and looked around to see where they were coming from. His eyes fixed on a single set of bleachers. Andy, wearing his Saints' uniform, held an air horn in one hand and a can of soda in the other. A cooler full of soft-drink cans sat beside him.

"Hey Paulie, catch!"

Andy pitched full cans of soda at his brother, one right after the other. No matter how hard Paul tried to avoid them, the cold cans kept slamming into his head.

Paul felt trapped! He couldn't move! Andy just laughed as the barrage continued. Paul watched in horror as a can flew straight at his face. Closer and closer and closer . . . .

Paul called out in his sleep and awoke with a start. It was daylight, wherever he was. Then it came back to him. He was in the hospital. Mom stood over his bed, clutching the book she had been reading.

"What's wrong, sweetheart?"

Paul scrubbed at his eyes with the back of his hand. "Nothin'. It was just a nightmare. Sorry."

"Do you need anything?"

"Maybe some water."

"Here you go," she said. She handed him a cold plastic mug of water with a bendable straw. He drank more than half of it before setting it on the tray his mother had just rolled in front of him.

"What time is it?" Paul asked.

"Almost eight o'clock. They'll be bringing your breakfast pretty soon."

There was a knock on the door.

"Someone's here to see you, Mr. Stewart! Are you decent?" A cheerful young aide said.

At the words "Mr. Stewart," his mystery visitor giggled in the hallway. Paul recognized Rachel's laugh. The door opened and Rachel, her mother, and Lisa walked in. Lisa carried a potted plant, and Rachel held onto a ridiculously large bouquet of balloons that said, "Happy Anniversary."

"Paul!" Rachel said. "How are you?"

"Yeah," said Lisa. "You look terrible."

"Lisa!" Mrs. Cassidy said.

"It's okay, Mrs. Cassidy," Paul said, smiling. "I bet I look pretty bad. Don't I, Rachel?"

"Maybe just a *little* like Frankenstein," she said.

"Actually," Paul said. "Frankenstein was the doctor who *created* the monster."

"Exactly," Lisa added. "The actual monster doesn't have a name."

"Looks like you and Lisa have a lot in common, Paul," Mrs. Cassidy said.

Paul felt bad. He hadn't meant to come off as a know-it-all like Lisa. He looked at Rachel to see how she felt. She was smiling.

"Glad to see your brain hasn't been damaged too bad," Rachel said. "Here. We got you some balloons."

"What anniversary are we celebrating?"

"Oh, that," Lisa said, grinning. "We were in a hurry and didn't have time to wait for the lady at the store to blow any up. So we took these."

Mrs. Stewart looked at her watch. "In another five hours or so, it will be twenty-four hours since you were conked on the head."

"Good enough for me," Rachel said. "These

balloons mark the almost one-day anniversary of the Soccer Soda War, of which Paul here is a casualty."

"Where's Andy?" Lisa asked.

"He and his dad are down in the cafeteria getting something to eat," Mom said. "We were waiting for sleepyhead to wake up. A few minutes ago I sent them down for breakfast."

"You must be exhausted," Mrs. Cassidy said. "Let me buy you a cup of coffee. The girls can visit with Paul for a little while."

"Actually, Mom, would you mind if I came too?" Lisa asked. "I'd like to check on Andy. I know he feels terrible about all of this. Do you mind, Paul?"

"No problem," he said, already feeling a little worn out from all the company. It would be nice to have a few minutes alone with Rachel. She tied the balloons to a chair and handed him a card. "Thanks, but I can't read it right now. I'm not supposed to strain my eyes."

"Well, I guess I'd better leave before my dazzling beauty blinds you for life," she said. They laughed together.

Paul hadn't noticed before, but Rachel also carried a gift bag.

"What's that?" he asked.

"Here," she said, pulling out a stuffed teddy bear in a soccer uniform.

"Now all we need is a mini can of pop to throw at

its head, and it'll look just like me," Paul said.

She took some tape from the tray and wrapped it around the bear's head. "Now you're twins," she said.

Paul laughed.

"Speaking of twins," she said. "I heard it was Andy who started the whole Soccer Soda War."

"Is that what they're calling it?" Paul asked.

"Yep. It was the headline in this morning's paper."

"It wasn't Andy's fault, totally," Paul said. "The whole game was out of control. The Warriors' fans were terrible, and one guy kept blowing an air horn during critical plays. Andy finally let the guy get to him."

"Are you mad at him? Has he apologized to you?"

"Actually," Paul said, "I haven't even seen him yet." Paul didn't know if he was mad at his brother or not. He didn't know how he felt. All he knew was that things between them had finally gotten completely out of control.

"Lisa and I had a long talk last night," Rachel said.

"Huh?" Paul felt like he had missed something and wasn't sure if he'd dozed off for a minute.

"After we heard what happened, Lisa came to my room," Rachel said. "As you well know, she and I don't have the best relationship. But she and Andy have gotten pretty close, and she knew I was, well, friends with you."

Paul didn't understand why Rachel looked so

uncomfortable. Weren't they friends?

"So, what happened?" Paul asked.

"She came to apologize to me," Rachel said.

"For what?"

"She told me that Andy had talked to her a lot about you. Evidently, Andy thinks you're, like, brilliant. He's really intimidated by you."

"Who, me?"

"Hang on," Rachel said. "I'll get to that. Anyway, this got Lisa to thinking. She realized that maybe I feel the same way around her that Andy does around you."

"Okay, I know I just suffered major head trauma, but you've totally lost me," Paul said.

"My whole life, I've thought Lisa was the smart one—the one who would be really successful. I knew she didn't hang out with friends as much as I did, but I thought it was because she was just too serious to do the dumb stuff my friends and I did. This whole time, she's been jealous of me."

"*I* could have told you that," Paul said.

"Really?"

"Yeah. Remember your dazzling beauty?" He grinned.

"Whatever. What I'm trying to tell you is that the reason Lisa's been so nasty to me is that she's been jealous of me, not because she thinks she's *better* than me," Rachel said. "I think things are going to be a lot better between us now. I mean, we may never be best friends, but I can tell things are different."

"That's great," Paul said, meaning it. "But I'm still not sure what that has to do with me and Andy."

"Don't you see? You're Lisa, and I'm Andy."

"Okay. That cleared it right up for me."

"I was afraid of that. This part isn't so easy for me to explain. You see, the reason Andy is so hard on you is that . . ." she paused.

"*Tell* me."

"You make him feel really stupid, like Lisa did to me," Rachel said quietly.

"What?"

"Before you get mad, just promise me you'll think about it, okay?" Rachel said.

Paul's head pounded with pain. It was just too much to think about. Paul just wanted her to go.

"I'm feeling pretty tired, and I've got a major headache, Rachel. Maybe you should go now. The doctor said I should get plenty of rest."

He could tell by the look on her face that he'd hurt her feelings, but right then, he didn't care.

"Sure," she said. "I'll, um, talk to you soon."

Paul held his head between both hands to keep it from spinning off, and it just wasn't the pain of the accident. Rachel was way out in left field. It wasn't his fault that he and Andy didn't get along. It was Andy's.

Andy was the jerk. It was Andy who hurt Paul, not the other way around.

But something deep down inside Paul told him that Rachel had hit pretty close to home. Memories from the past, like scenes from a movie, played in his head. The different reading groups. Paul's higher test scores. The thousands of times Paul had called Andy a moron or an idiot. Paul never thought Andy cared about any of that. What if he did? What kind of person did that make Paul?

Dr. Manning kept Paul in the hospital another night to run some more tests, "just to be sure." Sure of *what*, Paul didn't know. His head still hurt, but he wasn't quite as dizzy.

His room looked like a wedding reception, with flower arrangements and fruit baskets piled on every available surface, from his bedside table to the windowsill. Even Gavin, Topher, and Stephen had brought him a tray of cookies.

In the chair next to his bed, Paul's dad sat quietly reading the newspaper. Andy and Mom were at school picking up the assignments they'd both missed. It made Paul feel safe to have his dad nearby, even though they had never really clicked. Dad seemed to get along much better with Andy than he did Paul. But Paul loved his dad and enjoyed spending time with him. Getting hit on the head with a soda can just didn't seem like the most practical way of encouraging father/son bonding.

Paul tapped his fingers on the covers and sighed, so bored he couldn't stand it. "Dad, would it bug you if I turned on the TV?"

"No problem. Do you want me to do it for you?" his dad asked.

"No thanks, just find me the remote."

His dad looked around and finally spotted it attached to a chain, hanging down the side of the bed.

"Here you go."

Paul flipped through the channels, but there was nothing on. So he clicked it off, shut his eyes, and drifted off to sleep.

An hour later, Paul awoke again, this time hungry for something. His dad hit the call button for the nurse's station, and the aide brought him a cup of vegetable soup and some crackers.

While Paul slurped his soup, he thought about what Rachel had said to him about Andy. He wanted to ask his dad about it, but they'd never really talked about anything really important. Paul didn't know how to start, so he just blurted it out.

"When Rachel Cassidy was here, she said the craziest thing."

"What's that?" his dad asked.

"You'll laugh," Paul said, hoping he was right. "She said the reason Andy and I don't get along is that Andy is intimidated by me."

His dad was quiet for a minute. "I don't know, Paul. That doesn't seem so funny to me."

"Oh. Anyway, she also said that I'm too hard on Andy. That I make him feel stupid."

"You know," his dad said. "There is something funny about that."

"Really?" Paul said, feeling relieved. "What?"

"That you listened to Rachel tell you the same thing your mom and I have been trying to say to you for the past three years."

"Oh, come on, Dad!" Paul said, his temper flaring. "You've seen how Andy treats me."

"Yes, I have. He's hard on you, and I understand why you don't like it."

"You don't understand anything," Paul said. "You've always liked Andy better. You always take his side."

"Look, Paul, maybe now isn't the time—"

Once the emotion-charged words started gushing out, Paul couldn't stop them.

"No, now is the perfect time!" Paul said. "I'm in the hospital because of what Andy did. Not the other way around! Andy's the one who gets all the attention. Andy's the one with the anger problem. Andy's the one who bullies me and my friends at lunch every day.

He's the one who's made my life miserable for the past three years and can do no wrong, according to you. Andy's the problem here. Not me!"

Paul's head pounded, and he was seeing spots in front of his eyes.

"Paul," his father said, reaching over and taking his hand. "I had no idea you felt this way."

"Well, now you know."

"May I say something?" Dad asked.

As far as Paul could remember, it was the first time his father had ever asked him for permission to do anything.

"Fine," Paul said.

"If I've made you think I cared more about Andy than I do about you, I'm sorry. I worry about Andy more. Paul, you're so smart. And your mother and I are so proud of you. No matter what career choice you make, you have the right stuff to make it. You could be a doctor, or an attorney, or even a corporate executive. We can't wait to see what you're going to do with your life.

"But Andy really struggles, more than you know. School is a huge effort for him, and he's never going to do as well academically as you. You may not be aware of it, Paul, but the way you constantly pick on him makes it worse. The main key to success is confidence, and your insults about Andy being a moron took away most of his. He didn't have much to begin with."

"So what if I'm smart?" Paul asked. "Who cares? Andy's athletic. He's popular. Everyone likes him."

"I never knew before how much this bothered you," his dad said, sadly. "I know how much it hurt Andy— he's even talked to me about it a few times—but you always seemed to let it roll off your back."

"Because if I didn't, Andy would punch me. Besides, I did talk to Mom about it."

His dad sighed and looked down at the speckled vinyl floor before looking back at Paul. "She brought it up a couple of times, but I thought she was being overprotective." His dad smiled. "She has that tendency in case you hadn't noticed."

"Only about twenty times a day," Paul said.

"You know? That Rachel Cassidy might really be on to something."

"You mean about me and Andy?" Wincing with pain, Paul rubbed his forehead. It felt like someone was playing a bass drum in his head.

"Among other things." Dad smiled. "You get some rest now. We'll talk about this more later."

"Dad?"

"Yes, Son."

"Are you really proud of me?"

"More than you'll ever know, Paul. More than you'll ever know."

CHAPTER:08

When Dr. Manning made his hospital rounds early the next morning, he told Paul that he would be released in a few hours. Paul couldn't believe how much he wanted to get home into his own bed.

"But I want you to take it easy for the next week or two," Dr. Manning said. "Come in for a follow-up appointment next Monday. Have your mom call my office and schedule a time. You'll be playing soccer again before you know it."

"Great! Thanks, Dr. Manning."

Now all he had to do was wait for his mom to come pick him up around eleven o'clock. His dad had gone in to work to check his phone messages and respond to email, but he had told Paul he would be home early. He didn't know about Andy, whether he'd gone to school or not.

Paul still hadn't seen his brother since the accident. Andy had been in his room several times, but Paul had always been asleep when he came to visit. Which was okay by Paul, but now he was nervous about seeing Andy again.

Later that morning, fully dressed and propped up in bed, Paul leafed through a new soccer magazine. He was more than ready to go home. A small plastic sack held the free stuff the hospital gave him, plus all his magazines and Rachel's teddy bear gift.

When someone rapped on the edge of his doorframe, he thought it was Mom. Instead, in walked Andy.

"Hey," Andy said.

"Hey, yourself," Paul said. "Where's Mom?"

"She's at the nurse's station, making sure all your paperwork is in order. I think she had a few questions for Dr. Manning too."

"Oh," said Paul. He'd never felt so nervous around Andy before. Scared, yes. Nervous, no.

"So does your head still hurt?" Andy asked.

Paul started to say, "What do you think, you moron?" But caught himself. Instead he just said, "Yeah. The doctor said it could hurt for a few days from the concussion, and then the bruising on my head could hurt longer than that."

"Paulie, I'm really sorry it happened," Andy blurted out. "I wish it hadn't happened to you. I really do."

Paul knew he should accept Andy's apology, but he just couldn't. Not yet. He was still too angry. "Hey, don't start crying and expect me to just say everything is fine. It's not fine, Andy. Not by a long shot. None of this would have happened if you hadn't kicked that ball."

"I knew it was pointless to try to talk to you," Andy said. "You're always right." He turned to leave.

"I guess you'd rather punch me than talk to me."

Andy paused, then turned around again. "You know, I may not be as smart as you, but I'm not stupid, no matter how much you try to make me think I am. I came here because I needed you to forgive me for my part in the stuff that happened at the game. But it wasn't all me then, and the problems between you and me aren't all my fault either." He left the room.

A few minutes later, Paul's mom bustled through the door. "Okay, we're all set. As soon as the orderly comes with a wheelchair, we can get you out of here."

"Wheelchair?" Paul asked. "I can walk."

"Hospital rules. They made me ride in a wheelchair when I left the hospital after you and Andy were born. I held one of you in each arm. You were so tiny and perfect. It took your father and me thirty minutes to get to the car, because everyone in the hospital wanted to stop and see the twins. Where is Andy, anyway?"

"I figured he was with you," he said.

"Oh, that's right," she remembered. "I gave him the car keys. We'll just meet him outside."

After Mom drove the minivan home, she and Andy

gingerly helped Paul out of the front seat and each held an arm until he could collapse on the sofa in the family room. In retrospect, he was grateful for the wheelchair at the hospital, because the walk into the house had exhausted him.

"You need anything, Paulie?" she asked. Before he could answer, the phone rang, and his Mom went to the kitchen to answer it. A few minutes later Paul heard her hang up the phone.

"Andy," she said. "I need to talk to you and Paul. Why don't you come into the family room?" She sounded calm, but Paul could tell something was wrong. Andy sat down on the arm of the sofa, and Mom sat on the edge of the coffee table.

"That was Coach Benedict," she told the boys. "He called to check on Paul. Paul, I don't know if you remember, but he came by your room at the hospital several times, and that bouquet of flowers over there is from him and his wife."

"That's really nice," Paul said.

"That's not all he called about," she said. "The league called him to say that the Saints and the Warriors are each suspended from two weeks of games, effective immediately."

"There goes our shot at the division championship," Andy said, disgusted. He planted his hands on his knees and looked down at the beige carpet.

"There's more. They want a public apology from you Andy to the man you kicked the ball at, and they want a written apology from the team coach to all of the other teams in the league, with an assurance nothing like this will ever happen."

"What does Coach Benedict want me to do?" Andy asked, looking up.

"He'd like you to apologize. He's already agreed to send apology letters to all of the other teams. But he said the Warriors are refusing to apologize, which means they're out of the league."

"What does air horn man have to do?" Andy asked.

"He's barred from all future league soccer games," she said. "Which isn't as much as he deserves."

"I'll apologize," Andy said. "But it doesn't seem fair that our whole team should be penalized. If anyone should be suspended, it should be just me."

"I know this is hard, Andy, but you're dad and I'll be there for you."

"Can I go do my homework?" Andy asked.

"Sure." Andy jumped to his feet and strode down the hallway to their room.

Without saying anything, Mom brought Paul a glass of orange juice and the remote. "If you're set, I'll go check the mail."

While she was gone, Paul tuned into one of the

sports channels. She came back with a stack of cards.

"Autograph requests?" he said with a smile.

While the TV droned in the background, Paul read through the cards. He opened one from Coach Benedict, one from Will, and one from Mitch, who had been by the hospital a couple of times, but always when Paul was asleep. He even got a card from his homeroom teacher.

Along with the mail, his mother had added to the stack the cards he received in the hospital. There were two from Rachel. This one had been mailed to him after her hospital visit. Paul wondered if she was mad at him. On the front of the card was a beautiful blue sky full of puffy white clouds, with beams of light shining through. Inside, Rachel had handwritten a personal note. On the right was a scripture verse that read: *"If you forgive others, you will be forgiven"* (Luke 6:37 NLT).

Paul studied the verse before reading Rachel's note. How could he know for sure? If he decided to forgive Andy for everything he had done to Paul, how could he be sure that Andy would forgive him and stop being such a jerk?

Then he read Rachel's note.

Dear Paul,

I'm sorry you got hurt, and I'm sorry if you're mad at me for what I said about you and Andy. I hope you can forgive me. And I hope you and Andy can find a way to forgive each other. I've been angry at Lisa for such a long time. But when I think of how much Jesus has forgiven me for, I realize that he doesn't ask that much of me when he tells me to forgive her for what she's done to me.

I hope we're still friends. You're a really special person.
Your friend, Rachel

Paul thought about everything that had happened in the past three days. The accident. The things Rachel said. His talk with Dad. What he'd said to Andy at the hospital. Now this.

For the first time, Paul began to see things clearly. Yes, Andy had been a real jerk, but Paul wasn't any better—and Paul was the one who claimed to be a Christian. Paul knew the only thing to do was pray. He closed his eyes and put his full attention on God.

Lord, please forgive me for being so proud and stubborn and clueless, he prayed. *I should have accepted Andy's apology. I need to do some apologizing myself. Thanks for Rachel. She was the first one who told me the truth about Andy. Help me to be a better friend and a better brother. In Jesus' name, Amen.*

Later that day, after Paul took a nap in his own bed, he rolled over and saw Andy sitting on the tree house deck. Paul lifted up the window and yelled through the screen.

"Hey Andy, whatcha doin'?"

"Playing tennis," Andy said. "What does it look like?"

"Listen, I need you to come in and talk to me for a minute. I'd come out there but I'm not even supposed to climb stairs on my own. Will you...please?"

"If crocodiles don't eat me on the way."

Paul propped himself up on his pillows and waited for Andy, while his heart thumped loudly in his chest. This wouldn't be easy.

Andy slouched through the bedroom door and sat down on the edge of his bed. He hadn't said a word.

"I guess the crocodiles weren't hungry," Paul said, hoping to break the ice.

"Whatever. What do you want?"

"Look at this card Rachel gave me," he said. "Read the verse inside."

Andy read it to himself, stopping to examine it a couple of times.

"Not what I'd expect in a get-well card from a girlfriend," he said, handing the card back to his brother. "But it's got a nice picture."

"She's not my girlfriend," Paul said.

Paul could tell Andy was nervous. He was too. But he couldn't stand the thought of three more years, or three more days, living in an armed camp, barely speaking to one another. He decided to lay it all out. Andy would just have to listen.

"There's something I've really wanted to talk to

you about," Paul said. "This card just made me realize it's the right time. I'm not sure why we stopped being good friends. But I miss it, Andy."

Paul paused, hoping Andy would say something. He didn't. He didn't even look at Paul.

"You just make me feel so useless," Paul continued. "In gym class you always make fun of me. Up until a few games ago, you would make fun of me in soccer. Then when Coach Benedict put me in, it seemed to make you really mad. I know I'm not built like you, Andy, but I'm not that bad at sports, especially soccer. What I guess bugs me is that I feel like you want me to always fail."

"Really?" Andy said with a hint of sarcasm in his voice. "That's funny. Because you seem pretty determined for me to fail. Do you remember back in fifth grade? It was at the beginning of the school year. It was the fall right after I broke my arm. I spent most of the summer inside watching TV. Mrs. Walton split the class into reading groups, and you got into the highest one, and I got put in the lowest. That day at recess, you made fun of me in front of the whole class. You called me Turtle, because I was so slow. I couldn't figure out why you would embarrass me like that unless you were right. All I knew was that I was bad at school, but good at sports.

"It was something I could do better than you,"

Andy continued. "So I wanted to be in it alone. That way, Mom and Dad could be proud of you for your schoolwork, and I'd get some attention for my sports. Then you started getting better at sports, but I wasn't getting better at school."

"But it's not just sports you're good at, Andy. You're popular. Everyone likes you."

"Everyone is afraid of me, you mean," Andy said.

"What about Jimmy Hong? What about Tim?"

"Jimmy and Tim just hang out with me because I'm good at soccer. And you've got Rachel and all the other little angels at your youth group. The only person who's ever been nice to me is Lisa Cassidy."

Andy looked out the window at the tree house. Paul followed his gaze.

"Paulie, you know what was so great about hanging out with you when we were kids?" Andy asked.

"No, what?"

"We played on the same team. We looked out for each other. I remember when you stuck up for me at that soccer game when we were seven."

"And I'll never forget the time you got my lunch money back from Mack Hurley," Paul said.

"All it took was a well-placed snowball."

"He had a lump on his head for a week!" Paul said, laughing.

They both were quiet for a minute. "So all that

changed because I made fun of your reading group?"
Paul asked.

"It wasn't just that. It was like you were suddenly out to get me, to make me look stupid. Maybe you're right. Maybe I did turn into a jerk. But honestly, I just didn't even want to be around you."

Paul knew it was time for all this to end. "Andy, you're not the first person to tell me some of this stuff. In fact, there's been a long line of people the past few days. And I'm beginning to think you're right. I've been a real jerk to you."

"I don't want us to be enemies all our lives," Andy said. "Not even another day. So listen, I'm really sorry about your concussion and the other stuff at the game. I'm sorry for picking on you because you aren't the best athlete. Will you forgive me?"

"Sure, but I'm the one who needs to be forgiven," Paul said. "I'm sorry I ever made you feel stupid or dumb. And I'm sorry I called you a moron all the time. Will you forgive me?"

"Sure," Andy said, grinning.

"Can I ask you another question?" Paul asked.

"Since we're in the middle of an honesty-fest. Seems like a good time."

"Is that why you stopped coming to youth group? Because I made you feel dumb?"

Andy looked down at his fingernails. "You knew all

the answers in Sunday school. You could look up Bible verses before I could even remember if they were in the Old or New Testaments. And then, whenever I'd get called on to read a verse out loud, you'd make fun of me if I mispronounced anything. I just got sick of it."

"Andy, I'm really sorry," Paul said. "I think it's cool you've been coming to youth group again. I thought you quit because we were all nerds."

"Well, it's definitely nerdy," Andy said, but he was grinning.

Just then, their dad walked in. "Who wants Taco Casa take out?"

Both boys grinned widely and high-fived each other. Their dad looked puzzled, but pleased.

On Saturday morning Andy dressed out for soccer, even though the team couldn't play for the next two weeks. Coach Benedict still wanted the team to practice. Paul wanted to go along and put on a pair of khaki shorts and a T-shirt.

"I don't know if this is such a good idea, honey," his mom told him when she saw him dressed. "I doubt the doctor will even let you play again this season."

"I really want to be there," he said. "And I want to hear what Coach has to say."

"Okay," she said. "Tell you what, I'll stay around in the van. If you get tired you can just lay down and rest."

Paul wanted to roll his eyes. She was so

overprotective. But he realized that this time she might be right. He still felt a little weak.

As Andy and Paul bailed out of the minivan, they both noticed that several of the other guys weren't there, including Jimmy Hong.

"Where is everybody?" Paul whispered to Andy as they approached Coach Benedict and the remaining team members.

"Okay," Coach said. "Looks like everybody's here. Paul, it's good to have you. How's your head?"

"It hurts, but less than it did," he said.

"Glad you're doing better. You all may have noticed we're missing a few players. Several parents felt like it was in their children's best interest to no longer play for the Saints. They feel we haven't exactly lived up to our name this season."

Several people looked at Andy, who looked down at the grass.

"No offense, Coach, but why should any of us be here?" Derek asked. "I mean, there are only four games left in the season, and we're suspended for two of them. We've lost half our players. There's no way we can make it to post season."

"Is that how the rest of you feel?" Coach asked.

Except for Andy and Paul, everyone nodded.

"What about you, Andy?" Coach asked.

"The league already thinks we're bad sports. I

know I'm mostly to blame for that. But I don't want everyone to think we're sore losers too. I say we play our games and do the best we can."

"Andy's right," Paul said. "Besides, if we forfeit those games, the Saints will be out of the league next year too. Right Coach?"

"That's right. Looks like someone's been studying the league rule book. Shouldn't surprise me that it's you, Paul," Coach Benedict said.

"Actually," Paul corrected him, "it was Andy who read that part."

Paul realized that it was the first time in years he'd given Andy credit for anything. It felt pretty good.

"Come on, guys," Andy said. "What do you say?"

"How can we play?" Jeff Busch asked. "We don't even have enough players!"

The coach scratched his head. "I don't quite know what to do about that. I've talked personally to each of the parents involved, and they're pretty firm."

"What if I talked to them, Coach?" Andy asked. "I guess I owe them an apology too."

"Andy, you weren't totally to blame for what happened last week, and I don't want you to be too hard on yourself. But if you're willing to talk to those parents, it might make a difference."

Paul was stunned. Who was this guy? He thought he knew Andy pretty well, despite all their differences.

Andy hated talking to strangers, especially adults. Was he really willing to do this for the team?

Paul watched on the sidelines as Coach ordered the guys to run sprints. There weren't enough players for a scrimmage. For once Paul was actually grateful for his head injury. He always hated coach's drills. He found a spot on the grass and sat down to watch.

After practice, Andy collapsed next to Paul, breathing hard. "Those things kill me," he said breathlessly.

"And you always acted like I was a baby when I got winded!" Paul said.

"You are my baby brother," Andy said, grinning.

Coach Benedict came over to the two of them. "I just wanted to say again, Paul, how sorry I am this happened to you. More than anybody on the team, you've set an example of good sportsmanship this season."

"Thanks," Paul said.

"Andy, you too. I'm really proud of you for owning up to your part in what happened. I know it takes a lot of guts to make a public apology, much less talk to angry parents. Let me know if there's anything I can do to help."

"I've gotta do this on my own," Andy said. "But thanks."

"You're welcome. So, Paul, do you think you'll be

back to play with us next season? We'd love to have you as a starter."

"Thanks, Coach," Paul said. "That's really nice." He paused and looked at Andy. What would Andy think if Paul played soccer next year? "But I think I may get back on the academic team instead."

"You've got to be kidding!" Andy said. "You've got to play next year. You're the best forward in the league."

"I think any team would be lucky to have either Stewart on its roster," Coach Benedict said.

The brothers smiled at one another.

The next day, Paul and Andy sat with their parents during church. Paul didn't see Rachel. Sometimes she went to an earlier service. He hadn't had the chance to tell her yet how much her card had meant to him and that he wasn't mad at her anymore.

After church, the Stewart family headed for the soccer field as usual. But this time, Paul and Andy didn't need to go home and change first.

"Are you sure you wouldn't like to put on something more comfortable?" their mother asked.

"No thanks, Mom. I need to look nice for my public," Andy said with a wry smile.

Paul could tell Andy was really nervous. And this time, Paul had no idea how to help him.

They all got out of the minivan and walked across the grass toward the stands. A small podium with a microphone had been set up in front of the stands.

"You'll look just Pastor Jamison," Paul whispered.

Andy decided to wait behind the bleachers until it was time for him to speak. He didn't really want to see anyone or talk about anything. Paul stayed with him while their parents found seats.

"Hey, Andy," Paul said. "Do you remember our first soccer practice? When we were seven?"

"Yeah," Andy said. "You made the coach think you were the one who messed up so he wouldn't yell at me."

"I wish I could do something like that for you now," Paul said.

"There is something you could do," Andy said.

Paul was curious. "What?"

Andy looked embarrassed. "Um…would you pray for me?"

Trying not to show how surprised he was, Paul said, "Sure. I should have thought of that myself. Sometimes I can be really stupid."

"That's funny," said Andy. "I thought I was the stupid one."

"You know you're not stupid," Paul said. "And you're one of the bravest people I know."

"Maybe brave people are just too stupid to be afraid," Andy said. "I don't care. I just know I need help to get through this, and God is the only one who can help me right now."

"Okay," Paul said. He hadn't actually figured out what he might pray. "Here goes. Dear God, Andy really needs your help right now. He's really sorry about what happened. He wants to do the right thing. But he's nervous about apologizing to all those people who might be really mad at him and think he's a big jerk."

Andy interrupted him. "You're not exactly helping."

"Sorry." Paul continued to pray. "Please give Andy courage, Lord. Help him know what to say. Help all the players to play well and be safe today during the game. And thank you that my brother and me are friends again."

"My brother and *I*," Andy corrected.

"My brother and I," Paul repeated. "In Jesus' name, Amen." He looked at Andy. "Since when did you become the grammar guru?"

"Hey, I learned from the best," Andy said.

The buzzer sounded, signaling five minutes until the start of the game. It was Andy's cue.

"Thanks for the prayer, Paulie," Andy said.

"Anytime."

The brothers walked around to the front of the field. Andy stepped up to the podium, while Paul found his parents and sat down. Paul was surprised to see Rachel and Lisa sitting with his parents. He smiled, but he didn't have time to talk to either of them. Andy opened a folded sheet of paper and looked over at Coach Benedict, who was standing nearby. The coach nodded his head, and Andy began.

"Fellow soccer league players, family and friends, my name is Andy Stewart. I am on the Cedar Brook Saints. Last week, an incident occurred between our team and the Westmont Warriors. Because of some reckless pranks on the field, including a kick I made, the fans got involved. Unfortunately, innocent people were hurt. My brother Paul received a concussion from a can that was thrown from the stands. He won't be playing soccer again this season. But I have to accept the responsibility for it. If I hadn't lost my temper, none of this would have happened. On behalf of my team and my coach, I want to apologize for our part in this incident. Once the league lifts our suspension, we promise to return as better players, sportsmen, and people. Thank you."

Andy lowered the paper and turned to leave. His coach gave him a pat on the back.

"Well done, Andy," Coach Benedict said. Andy climbed the bleachers to sit beside Paul. When he saw Lisa, he smiled.

"Do you guys want to stay for the whole game?" their dad asked.

"I think we should," Andy said. "It would be rude to leave now."

Paul knew Andy was right, but he was anxious to talk to Rachel alone. Instead he watched as the Springfield Rockets beat the Shelbyville Hornets. The game wasn't even close. Paul felt a little bad for the Hornets, especially the goalie, who looked worn out from all the goal attempts, few of which he was able to stop.

When the game was over, Paul turned to Andy first. "You did a really good job."

"Your prayer really helped," he said. "I was terrified. But when I got behind the podium, I felt this total peace."

"God was right there with you, man," Paul said. "That's awesome."

"Now I only have to do that at four more games this weekend."

"I'll be there with you, bro," Paul said. "From now on, all the time."

"Thanks, Paulie. Hey, I'm going to go catch up with Lisa. See you back at the van in a few minutes."

As Andy walked away, Paul looked around for Rachel. Standing next to a trash can, she picked up plastic bottles and sandwich wrappers people had left on the ground. He walked over to her.

"It drives me crazy that places like this don't have recycling bins," she said.

"Reduce, reuse, recycle. That's what I always say,"

Paul said.

"That's funny," Rachel said. "I've never heard you say that before."

"I meant, always, as of right now."

"At least you're talking to me. After what I said to you in the hospital, I wasn't sure we would be friends anymore."

"You made me pretty mad," Paul said. "But only because you were right. I've been wanting to talk to you all week and let you know that I think Andy and I have patched things up."

"I know," she said.

"How?" Paul asked, a little disappointed that he hadn't gotten to tell her himself.

"Andy called Lisa and talked to her for an hour on the phone the other night. Actually, they talk on the phone just about every day," Rachel said.

"You're kidding!"

"Nope. Some people actually like talking to their girlfriends on the phone. You should try it sometime."

"But I don't have a girlfriend," Paul said, unable to look Rachel in the eyes.

"Don't you?" Rachel smiled and they turned to walk toward the parking lot. When he slid in the backseat, she said, "See you at youth group."

"Yeah," Paul said, smiling. "See ya."